Braiswick (*division of Author Publishing Ltd*)
61 Gainsborough Road, Felixstowe,
Suffolk IP11 7HS,
www.author.co.uk

ISBN 1 898030 48 0

British Library Cataloguing in
Publication Data available.

Illustrations from original works of
art. Cover design by Cathi Stevenson

Produced in Milton Keynes
by Lightning Source

Acknowledgements

I would like to express my sincere
appreciation to everyone who helped me
with the creation of this book.

Dr Helena Grega and her assistant Cristina Matteus from the
Geographic Society of Lisbon;
Frank Valcarcel and his wonderful wife, Inez;
Dr Antonio Lopes Leao da Silva at the Institute of Scientific Tropical
Research in Lisbon;
The Museum of Ethnology, Lisbon;
Dr Fernanda Fernandes from The Cape Verdean Embassy in Lisbon;
Ray Cardoza, Onset, MA;
Waltraud (Traudi) Berger Coli, Cranston, RI;
Alfreida Faria Balla Cardoza, Wareham, MA;
Association Cabo-Verdiana, Lisbon (Francisco Antonio Tomar, Joao
Miranda, Elsa Fontes and the entire staff of the association);
The National Library, Lisbon; Arquivo Nacional da Torre do Tombo
(ANTT), Lisbon;
The municipality of Noli, Italy;
The University of Genova, Italy;
Biblioteca Museu do Finale, Italy, the Public Library of Noli, Italy;
The Municipal Library of Porto, Porto, Portugal;
CIDAC, Lisbon;
Glaucia Nogueira, Casa do Brasil, Lisbon.

These people and many more played a crucial role in making this
book possible. I would also like to thank the city of Lisbon which
hosted the 1998 Expo and which helped to give the world a better
understanding of the Portuguese speaking world and its history.
Fortunately one can find a diverse community in Lisbon and
throughout Portugal where it is possible to share a certain brotherhood
of Portuguese speaking nations and share in the discussions of culture
and history.
There is also a wealth of information in bookstores and libraries
regarding this history which I found to be fascinating.
Many thanks to all those who helped in this project. At times I must
confess that I wanted to quit, especially after depleting much of my
personal funds, since this project was the result of personal funds,
yet somehow, it is my sincere hope that these efforts which took years
in the making and thousands of miles in travel and at great sacrifice
to me personally, will benefit the reader who has an interest in this
history.
Hopefully I will build a data base in the future and will be able to

assist others in their efforts to trace this fascinating history.

In closing I would like to remind everyone that there are now many Portuguese speaking communities throughout the U.S. and around the world that are working together to promote and preserve this heritage. Anyone wishing to contact me for comments or questions may do so at email: marcelogomes@hotmail.com

Sincerely: Marcel Gomes Balla

Contents

Introduction 7
Volume l
Cabo Verde 13
Antonio da Noli and
Christopher Columbus 15
Brazil 35
Hispanic & Lusophone 41
Port Movement 55
Notable Personalities 59
Antonio da Noli 60
Diogo Afonso 61
Vasco da Gama 62
Henry Mendes 63
Captain John Sousa 64
Captain Jose Lima 65
Captain Joseph Manuel
Lopes 66
Almicar Cabral 67
Captain Pedro Evora 68
Columbus 69
Roberto Duarte Silva 70
Eugenio Tavares 71
Volume II
The Church 74
Roberto Duarte Silva 80
Impact on Trade 83
International Aid 87
The Jews 90
Historical Problems 91
Racial Problems 92
Unpublished Views 95

Other Islands 110
Andre Alvares
de Almada 112
Treaty of Tordesilhas 119
Royal Letters 133
The Geographical Axis of
History 136
Vasco da Gama's Secret 139
Spanish Involvement in the
Slave Trade 140
Slave Trade Routes 142
VOLUME III
The 'Missing Pages of Blacks
and Hispanics 145
Atrocities 146
Columbus Map 171
Juan de la Cose Map 173
Cape Verdean Organisations
174
Information 179
Monte Gordo 185
Comercial shipping 192
Cages 194
Populations of other
Lusophone communities 195
The Project "Luso Grande do
Sul" and the Discovery of
Brazil 500 years 197
Historical Items 201
Other Comments By
Lusophones 207
Unpublished Information
210

ABOUT THE AUTHOR

Dr. Marcel Gomes Balla is a graduate of Boston University with an MA in International Relations in 1976. He also studied at the University of Lisbon and other universities in Portugal. He has served abroad as an International Community Development consultant, speaks seven languages, has written many articles on the history of Cabo Verde, and has also given many lectures at various institutions throughout the U.S., Europe and the Middle East.

The author was raised in the town of Wareham, MA and could not understand why the teachings of his ancestral homeland was not included in the educational system, so he decided to embark on a course that would take more than 20 years of research, studying several languages and travel to four continents at a cost of many thousands of dollars of his personal funds in order to document this history. Finally he realized that the history of Cabo Verde represented the beginnings of a New World which would dramatically change the course of mankind forever. Now he simply wants the world to recognize the contributions of Cabo Verde and the Cape Verdean people to the history and development of the modern world.

1

Throughout his research he was amazed to discover the historical links to the 'Missing Pages' of Afro-American and Hispanic History. But that was not all, as the reader will learn, he uncovered the secret pages of maritime history for the Italians, the Portuguese and Columbus in addition to many other secrets that are being exposed for perhaps the first time.

An earlier book by the author is **The "OTHER" Americans-** The True Story About America's Most Neglected Minorities. This book is an excellent prelude to a better understanding of this book.

If it is not available in your bookstore, you may make inquiries to the author – marcelogomes@hotmail.com or the publisher

Definitions of commonly used words or expressions

Lusophones: Approximately 200 million people who have their historical roots in Portugal or in any of her former colonies.

Hispanics: Approximately 300 million people who have their historical roots in Spain or in any of her former colonies.

New World: The world which had been unknown outside of Europe, the Middle East and Asia (the old world) by Europeans. This begins with the Atlantic Islands of the Azores, Madeira and Cabo Verde in the 15th century (Reference: The Shaping of America, Dr .D.W. Meinig,1986) (Novo Mundo)

UCCLA : The group of capital cities of the Portuguese speaking countries in America, Africa, Asia and Europe.

Ordem do Cristo : A religious military organization that succeeded the Ordem dos Templarios (The Order of the Templates) and financed the voyages of discovery by the Portuguese. Much of their history was conducted in secret so even today it is difficult to obtain the details of this history. The Infante D. Henrique, the third son of King D. João I, became the Grand Master of this organization in 1416 with a vision of circumnavigating Africa and reaching India, because of the Muslim control of the Mediterranean, this would be the only way to go.

CPLP : The commonwealth of the eight Portuguese speaking nations in America, Africa and Europe.

Lanzado: Mestizos who were descendants of Europeans and Africans, who became slave traders and practiced their trade on the Coast of Guiné, especially in the area of the Island of Goreé (today it is a part of Senegal).

3

New Christians: Iberian Jews who were involuntarily converted to Christianity

Mulatto: A word which usually means a person of mixed race, is taken from the word mula which means mule in several Latin languages. Since a mule is the off spring of a horse and donkey or two different breeds of animals. Thus a person of two different races, e.g. black and white has become a mule or mulatto in the Portuguese language. Often times mulatto and mestizo are used interchangeably between the two depending on the experience of the user.

Antonio's Island: The name of the discoverer of Cabo Verde (Antonio da Noli) was often used as a direct reference by cartographers and others for Cabo Verde. So on old maps one may see the name of Antonio's Island as well as that of Cabo Verde when representing this archipelago. For the purpose of reading this book, Antonio's Island means the same as Cabo Verde.

Cabo Verde and the Expansion of Western Civilization

In order to understand the history of the expansion of western civilization one must first recognize the history of Cabo Verde, a sea base, apparently fostering an extreme example of a European civilization in the middle of the ocean. This archipelago of 10 islands was obligated to supply international aid to various continents while expanding western values in these areas. Their navigators transported immigrants to many countries around the world Africans, Europeans, Hispanics, Cape Verdeans-everyone.

This book is complete with documentation recently revealed with secrets about:

- The 'official' discovery of Cabo Verde
- The Treaty of Tordesilhas- the complete text-in English
- The Cape Verdean navigator who made an extraordinary impact on America, Africa, Europe and Asia
- The involvement of the church with slavery
- The historical ties between Cabo Verde and Columbus
- Cabo Verde Vasco da Gama and Cabral
- The creation of Brazil
- The historical ties with Italy and other countries
- The first non-Europeans to cross the Atlantic with a regular sailing schedule and a lot more useful information such as:
- Portraits of Cape Verdean navigators published for the first time for the public (Africans , mestizos, Europeans, but always Cape Verdeans). Still other famous Cape Verdeans in science, politics etc.
- Maps to confirm the discovery of the islands and the importance of Cape Verdeans and Cabo Verde in world history.

5

- A list of Cape Verdean contacts in Europe, America and Cabo Verde.
- And still much more - a history that will undoubtedly surprise the world with its shocking revelations of the people and events that changed the course of world history forever.

APPENDICES
- Portraits of Great Navigators and other Famous Cape Verdeans
- The Church, Slavery and the Doctrine of Racial Superiority
- A Special Report on Roberto Duarte Silva a Famous Chemist
- The Cape Verdean Impact on International Trade
- Examples of International Aid
- The Jews and Cabo Verde
- Historical Problems with Race in America
- Views of Cabo Verde by Gaspar do Couto Ribeira Villas
- Maps
- The Treaty of Tordesilhas - the full text
- Royal Letters with Proof of the Discovery of Cabo Verde the first 5 islands - then the last 7 islands
- Cabo Verde, the Geographical Axis of History
- Vasco da Gama's Secret
- Cabo Verde and Spain in the Slave Trade
- Slave Ships
- Atrocities
- Cabo Verde and some Commemorative Stamps
- Cape Verdean Organizations Worldwide
- Tourist Information - Cabo Verde)
- Other Useful Information
- Travel Agencies - Culture Centers in Europe, Cabo Verde and the USA
- Miscellaneous
- Other Books to Read

Introduction

This special report is really a trilogy of the various aspects of the Cape Verdean impact on the world, especially the Western world and Africa.

It is divided in three parts based on the discovery of the islands and the achievements of the Genoese navigators Antonio da Noli and Christopher Columbus. Both of these navigators participated tremendously in the history of Cabo Verde with a great impact on civilization that resulted in the world we know today. Then the Cape Verdean impact on the discovery and transformation of Brazilian society, and finally the Cape Verdean impact on the African and Hispanic societies with ties to the Lusophone world.

All of these stories are tremendously important in the study of humanity over the last 500 years, because Cabo Verde was always in the center of the transformation of one of the most important phases in the history of mankind - the Discoveries. Therefore I shall begin with the introduction to shed some light on this history and its impact on the world.

After the discovery of the islands, Portugal used them to establish a logistics base between the 15th and 16th centuries to enforce her policies of overseas expansion. This era was before the intervention of Europeans on the coast of Africa (they were usually at war with one another in Europe during this period). Since the African coast is very extensive and flat it is very difficult to control. The land didn't offer any strategic outposts to control and defend the territory. At this time, strategic outposts in Africa could define political as well as economic authority in this area, whether in the interior or along the coast.

Portugal being a small country with limited resources, could not set up such outposts to control the African ports. Besides this, it would have been very dangerous and she could not maintain the military forces necessary to protect the administration with such extensive obligations. Thus the obvious solution was to make use of the Cape Verde Islands which are 500 kilometers from the coast of Africa, in order to manage these objectives. In this way Cabo Verde would be used as a fort in the ocean to control the politics and economy as well as scientific and geographical studies and so much more.

These islands would serve as a laboratory to experiment with farm products and the raising of horses and livestock. These Cape Verdean horses were well known and desired around the world, as was cotton in international trade.

According to Maria Santos, horses and cotton were already products of Cabo Verde before the year 1472.

The land is very difficult for agriculture, but still it would serve as an intermediary base, producing planting systems that would be transferred to other parts of the world. this was especially the case with Brazil. The Brazilian settlements were dependent on logistical support from Cabo Verde and the Cape Verdeans had a mandate from the King of Portugal to provide it.

With the transfer of slaves to the New World, the Cape Verdean impact would have several key features regarding the Indians as African manual labor would replace that of the Indians while allowing them to conserve a little more of their history. This is a fundamental point of this book, to be able to analyze the Cape Verdean impact on various aspects of mankind and the consequences that have resulted today. In this way we must begin to understand the relationship among different societies due to this impact. Because unfortunately there is a lot of animosity in today's world between different ethnic groups and these groups do not understand the details of their past, as this is a subject that is not taught in schools. But personally I have a lot of confidence in this area of education.

When people start to understand the circumstances of different ethnic groups, we can diffuse the xenophobia that exists among them now. How did the Africans come to America? Why was Cabo Verde designated as the point to control slavery? What role did the Spanish play in the slave trade destined for the new world? Where did the mestizo race begin? What was the Cape Verdean role regarding Hispanics and the beginning of their history in the New World? And what was the Cape Verdean role regarding the Lusophones? And regarding America? What was the church's role regarding

slavery? Did the church deal in the slave trade? In this short report I have tried to provide answers to all of these questions with supporting documentation.
Why is this so?

Because for the first time in the history of mankind we have the nucleus of a civilization at the center of the world where we can analyze and trace the history to a new civilization and a new human type that actually transformed the civilization of the world.

For this reason, I strongly believe that it is a subject that should be taught in schools worldwide, especially since in Cabo Verde there are influences from all over the world, because it was involved extensively on all continents: South America, North America, Europe, Africa and Asia as well as Australasia.

In reality Cabo Verde furnished international aid to different continents five centuries ago. This aid was extensive and there is plenty of documentation at the National Archives of Torre do Tombo in Lisbon to confirm this history.

For example, the Cape Verdean impact did not stop with the transfer of Africans five centuries ago to Latin America, but it was also a place that was nearly mandatory for the passage of Europeans going to Brazil and other South American countries in the 19th and 20th centuries. This aid was also extended to South Africa and Australia, especially for German, Italian and English emigrants among others.

We would like to see great countries recognize the contributions of Cabo Verde in their teaching of history. For example, countries, such as the USA and England have received the direct aid of Cape Verdeans many times and in Porto Grande there is a cemetery for sailors of the American and Royal Navies.

Even Commodore Perry relied on Cape Verdeans many times during his campaign to help Afro-Americans move to Liberia 150 years ago

(Ref: 'Old Bruin' by S. E. Morrison 1967).

We hope that one day these nations will be aware of these contributions that are usually hidden in the history of their countries (for example, known by historians but not taught in the school system). Ironically many Americans know that

9

American Blacks returned to Africa and settled in Liberia before the civil war in the United states, but practically none of them know that Cape Verdeans provided extraordinary help in obtaining their freedom in Africa at that time.

I hope that this information which is being revealed for perhaps the first time, the world will become aware of the Cape Verdean involvement that was always at the center of a major phase in the transformation of humanity. But we must understand that unfortunately there is plenty of controversy in this history. Yet, on the positive side we can see it as a study from which we can correct the mistakes of the past. Now there is much more interest in this subject as there are so many social problems. Fortunately there are people who would like to live in peace and be able to lead a normal life. Clearly, the xenophobia that exists in today's world is at a point that could destroy many societies. All because this subject is not taught in schools.

From a positive point of view, in the United States, the Smithsonian Institute has begun a program called 'The Cape Verdean Connection Program' to experience a society that blends. This program is very important , because with all the xenophobia that exists in the United States there are some people who would like to know how is it that Cape Verdeans can live harmoniously in their multiracial society without racial preconceptions.

It is also fortunate that Portuguese teachers of the Grupo de Trabalho do Minesterio da Educacao para as Comemoracoes dos Descobrimentos Portugueses are taking much more interest in this subject and have already published some books referring to the Portuguese discoveries such as 'Views about Cabo Verde' and they are preparing another book with the title 'Cabo Verde, Geografia e Historia'. In the meantime, at the end of this book there are some books listed referring to Cape Verdeans and the Portuguese which are important to the study of this subject. So I believe that the Portuguese are going to begin teaching this history in their scholastic system. A lot of people know a little about the history and the glory of Portugal during the Discoveries but practically no one knows that this history could not exist without the history of Cabo Verde because the glory began in these islands.

Thus the favorable areas to study in this history are:.

1 The first society that reached equality without racial preconceptions (clearly there are problems of poverty, but many such problems are a carry over from slavery from which there is now an evolution along with the progress of the nation). Generally speaking, in Cabo Verde, it is said that "cape verdeans have many faces but are one people". One can say that cape verdeans don't have racial preconceptions because the overwhelming majority of them are of mixed races, but there are plenty of blacks and a few whites. However, in practice the majority consider themselves as members of the human race because everyone is involved either directly or indirectly with everyone at all levels of society whether it be with family members or just with friends. We must remember that cape verdeans fought with the Africans in the war of independence and thus they have good relations on the African continent. At the same time we must remember that the majority of cape verdeans reside abroad and many of them are mixed with different nationalities. These are the very ones who provide economic assistance to those who remain on the islands. In their own way everybody depends on someone else for their survival. Therefore they must respect the rights of everyone.

2 The importance of the discovery of the Cape Verde Archipelago and the importance of the discoverer during this time-Antonio da Noli.

3 The importance of Cabo Verde amidst the creation of the Hispanic and Lusophone societies with an African base and then a European base.

4 The importance of international aid supplied by Cabo Verde with emphasis on those European emigrants who went to America, Africa and Australia.

5 The impact of Cabo Verde on America, especially with emphasis on the cotton industry and horses as well as the whaling industry, strawberries and cranberries among others.

6 The involvement of Cabo Verde with the discovery of a route to India and other famous Portuguese discoveries.

11

7 The direct involvement of Cabo Verde in European societies.

Clearly there is a lot more to study. Unfortunately this work is limited, but hopefully it will inspire historians to examine this subject in greater detail.

Reference: Emilia Madeira Santos, Strategic Islands, Centro de Estudos de Historia. Cartografia Antiga - Serie Separatas 212 IICT Lisboa, 1988

CABO VERDE, CABO VERDE

The sea, the sea has always been a part of you
and me,
we all were born of it and to return again, as
men of the sea
is our ultimate destiny.
A desire born of cultural pride that has forever
burned from deep inside me.
The sea surrounds us and unites us with that
universality of life's potentiality, never the
same from moment to moment always ready
to be another possibility, of creativity that
manifests life's dignity and multiplicity.
The sea runs through our veins and sustains
our communality, our universality. Who could
deny the reality of our multi-cultural society?
With dignity and pride we will forever abide
the continuing tide of ignorance and "mis-
history" of our reality. Like the seas that touch
all shores, we carry the blood of all people
from all shores, and more. A society likened to
a warm soup that warms the belly and lifts the
spirit on a cold night. Oh Cabo Verde, you
should be proud, be strong be forever the
human paradigm.
For soon the world will find that the key to the
mystery of all desires toward happiness is not
in how much you can get for yourself, but in
how much you can contribute to others.

13

Cabo Verde, Cabo Verde

The original multi-cultural society.
Born of colonial impropriety,
We have forever changed the world's destiny.

To all shores we have come
To show the world what has been done
in the name of prosperity
and religiosity.

We are the people who bear no animosity,
To those who have created this multiplicity.

For you see
We have proven that universality
Is a possibility
In a multi-cultural society

14

Antonio da Noli and Christopher Columbus

Many historians know little about one of the most important navigators in the history of navigation. His name is Antonio da Noli, a Genoese in the service of the Infante D. Henrique in Portugal during the 15th century. Da Noli was also known by the name Antonio Usodimare which was possibly his real name in Genoa. However, he came from a small town near Genoa known as Noli (or Nolla). In Portugal he was known as Antonio da Noli.

Antonio da Noli was the discoverer of the Cape Verde Islands in 1460 and later in 1462 he became the founder of the first Cape Verdean society in the city of Ribeira Grande on the island of Santiago as a citizen naturalized by the Infante D. Henrique.

This navigator was also a merchant as were many of the navigators of this era, including Columbus. And like Columbus, Antonio da Noli was also a map maker, in any case, he offered his services to Portugal, which were accepted, as Portugal was interested in recruiting good navigators for the development of sea routes along the African coast with the goal of finding a route to India.

In his service to Portugal he discovered the Cape Verde Archipelago around 1460. Many historians believe that this was the most important discovery in the life of the Infante and perhaps the last one. Unfortunately this discovery is embroiled in controversy in trying to determine the true discoverer with a correct date. Ironically this controversy exists only with the discovery of the Cape Verde Islands among the great Portuguese discoveries which number some twenty. The controversy is usually in deciding between Alviso Cadamosto, Diogo Gomes or Antonio da Noli with some arguments in favor of Vincent Dias and Diogo Afonso.

But now with new revelations of documents in Portugal and with more interest in this area, historians seem to accept da Noli as the discoverer. This conclusion is based on some documents that clearly show that da Noli discovered five islands in the archipelago of Cabo Verde: a royal letter dated 19 September 1462 attributes the discovery of five islands with the names - Santiago, Sao Filipe, Sao Cristovao, Sal and Maias, which were the names given to these islands at that time, but shortly afterwards these names were changed to:- Sao Tiago, Fogo, Boa Vista, Sal and Maio. In the royal letter, the Infante D. Fernando (the brother of D. Henrique) inherited the Cape Verde Islands after the death of D. Henrique in 1460, while nothing was mentioned about the other islands except to say that seven islands were discovered by the Infante (D. Henrique) with the names that still exist today - Raso and Branco (two islets), Santa Luzia, Santo Antao, Brava, Sao Nicolau and Sao Vicente. It is also of interest to note that in this same letter that states that the five islands were discovered by da Noli during the life of the Infante D. Henrique (he died in 1460). Another important observation is that the first five islands constituted a part of Guine and the last seven islands were a part of Cabo Verde *(see note 1)*.

Antonio da Noli was awarded the captaincy of the southern part of the island of Santiago and founded Ribeira Grande as the capital together with his brother and nephew. All of this information is important because da Noli received many privileges, including a title of nobility and Portuguese citizenship which were honors rarely given to foreigners during this period.

Some writers believe that da Noli discovered six islands because they can't imagine that a navigator could discover the island of Fogo without seeing the island of Brava, since Brava is very close to Fogo. But I discard this hypothesis because it is very possible that da Noli could have seen Fogo from a distance without sailing around it, thus he would not have seen Brava which is behind Fogo shielded by a great volcano which at nearly 3,000 meters high could have hidden Brava from any boats coming from Santiago. However, there is another theory that is probably more likely, that Brava is always mentioned in documents with the islands of Santo Antao, Sao Vicente, Sao Nicolau, Santa Luzia, Raso and Branco while it is actually located closer to Fogo, Santiago and Maio.

For this reason, there are those authors who make the argument that Brava was erroneously classified by administrators of the Kingdom and really was discovered by Antonio da Noli if he sailed around Fogo, and in this case this theory weighs a lot. We must also remember that with the death of the Infante, perhaps some time lapsed when there would have been some confusion especially since we know that the islands remained unsettled for two years after his death.

So, the great success of da Noli became legendary in Genoa and these stories would have reached aspiring navigators and merchants of that city creating a lot of interest, especially with merchants such as Columbus. Unfortunately, we do not find any documentation to verify any effect that these stories would have had on Columbus. Therefore we have to analyze the life of Columbus from the facts we know. It is well known that he was born in Genoa and was a young Genoese during the period of da Noli's achievements and certainly the fame of this navigator (da Noli) began to attract many Genoese to Portugal, who were interested in commerce and adventure. There was a lot of commercial interest in sugar from Portugal and Madeira and others were interested in these islands that had been recently discovered by the Portuguese in the Atlantic as well as the trade on the African coast of Guine.

Obviously these arguments are very important when we start to make the connection between trade and sugar. Why? Because there does exist one document that effectively shows that Columbus went to Portugal as a merchant to get a load of sugar for businessmen in Genoa with a date of 25 August 1479, in which it is stated that he was a Genoese national and had already been living in Portugal for a year and that he wished to return *(see note 2)*.

Our history has already taught us that Columbus' life is filled with mysteries and we also know that he learned the art of navigation in Portugal and lived in Madeira where he married a Portuguese woman from this archipelago. It is also generally accepted by historians that he most likely went along the African coast up to Guine and to Cabo Verde. According to the Encyclopedia Portuguesa Brasileira, the Madeirans had introduced sugar cane to Cabo Verde. We also know that Columbus developed the idea of sailing to India during this time. This era was between 1476 and 1485 according to the information in Portugal, where he was as a merchant and navigator. Eugene Lyon tells us in an article of National Geographic Vol. 181 No. 1, January 1992, titled: 'Search for Columbus', that he sailed along the African coast down to Sao Jorge da Mina (El Mina). His southern voyages were considered to be very useful as he had to make more than one trip with Genoese commerce between Portuguese Guine and the new Castillian colonies in the Canary Islands. So, Columbus demonstrated a knowledge of Cabo Verde, the Canaries and S. Jorge da Mina.

Columbus was in Noli in 1476 where he prepared for his voyage to Portugal and then was shipwrecked off the coast of Portugal but managed to make it safely to land. During this time, according to an article by Jack Altman in the book 'Berlitz-Italy Blueprint' 1989, Columbus spent time in the Azores, Madeira and Cabo Verde. Logically, if he spent a little time in Noli, he would have had the opportunity to meet da Noli's family. The truth is that in 1438 the only known cartographer in the Genoa area was Antonio da Noli's brother. This cartographer, Agostinho da Noli, was a specialist in making maps for navigators. Thus it is very possible that Columbus would have known him or at least he would have been aware of his works.

According to Alberto Viera, Columbus sailed to S. Jorge da Mina on the Guinean coast between 1482 and 1484 (based on the history of Bartolomeu de las Casas), it was probably during this time when he went to the Cape Verde Islands for the first time. We don't have much doubt about this story, because Columbus, himself, tells us that he was in Cabo Verde and had seen many frigate birds there *(Ref: his ship log of 29 September 1492, during his first voyage to America)* and therefore he believed that when he saw such birds in the sky overhead, he was approaching land because these birds were a sign that land was nearby.

Another story of equal significance was his hope to get to India by way of Cabo Verde because he already understood the trade winds in that area and he considered these to be very favorable to make such a trip. But unfortunately he didn't make it to Cabo Verde during his famous voyage because Portugal and Spain were at war at this time so he had to go by way of the Canary Islands. It is of interest to note that he finally went to Cabo Verde during his third voyage to America when Portugal and Spain were at peace in June 1498.

Why do we think that this story is important? As we already know, there are few documents to verify the life of Columbus between 1476 and 1485, the period in which he was most confident in his ideas of navigation. We can agree that he learned navigation in Portugal. Fine, but then what? Surely if there were many Genoese attracted to Portugal to learn the secrets of navigation and participate in the sugar business and the trade along the coast of Guine, based on the fame and stature of da Noli, then logically one can argue that Columbus also would have been influenced by da Noli. But what has not been said until now is that da Noli governed Ribeira Grande and the southern part of the island of Santiago while having a lot of influence over the commerce on the coast of Guine and a lot of interest in sugar, since sugar cane was one of the first products in Cabo Verde (coming from Madeira where Columbus had been involved in this business) and is still in operation today, especially on the island of Santo Antao. Perhaps, even more important was the fact that da Noli was also a Genoese and the most important navigator of this period in the service of Portugal while speaking the same language as Columbus since were bothGenoese.

Now we have to hypothesize a little. Logically we can say that Columbus could have been in Cabo Verde to learn the art of navigation and understand the importance of the trade winds in the area, so why not ask for help from an outstanding expert such as da Noli, who spoke the same language? In science this is called 'the law of natural attraction'. There were also other Genoese there, such as da Noli's brother Bartolomeu and his nephew Rafaelo as well as others from Genoa.

In his article in National Geographic Eugene Lyon tells us that when Columbus was in Lisbon he naturally established himself with the Genoese. Therefore it would have been very natural for him to establish himself with the Genoese in Cabo Verde. During this period the island of Santiago was well known in Lisbon as Antonio's Island and all the Genoese merchants had to know about Antonio da Noli because they were dealing in commerce between Guine and Cabo Verde and the Genoese were very active in the slave trade.

According to the book 'Le Americhe Annunciata' page 110 and 126 (note 17) the archipelago was called Antonio's Island or Cabo Verde which had already been noted on the map of Juan de la Cosa (1500), this is also found in the writings of Joao de Barros and Bartolomeu de las Casas.

Ref: 'L'Asia by J. de Barros pages 64/5' "We find that during this period the islands that are now known as Cabo Verde were discovered by Antonio da Noli a Genoese by nationality and a nobleman, because of being disgusted with his homeland, he came to this kingdom (Portugal) with two ships and a cargo vessel (typical of use in the Mediterranean) accompanied by his brother and nephew. The Infante (D.Henrique) gave them permission that would allow them to make discoveries and sixteen days after leaving Lisbon they anchored on the island of Mayo: they gave it this name because of the day that they arrived there (May 1st) and on the 2nd May they discovered two more islands, Santiago and San Filipe, then they discovered the other islands, totalling ten, while naming the group of islands Cabo Verde, because it was located about 100 leagues from the promontory on the African coast that bears that name, they were known by ancient geographers as the Fortunate Islands (as Fortunados) which is still used in our geography. The King transferred these to the Infante D. Fernando (D. Henrique's brother) in September of 1462: and the first island to be settled was known as Santiago and the King gave him (da Noli) the right

20

to do business in Guine with more freedom than the king desired. In another letter he was given restrictions which were more in line with the King's original intentions."

So I believe that there are strong arguments to connect the discovery of America directly or indirectly with the influence of the first resident Cape Verdean, a nobleman who was naturalized as a citizen by D. Henrique.

Now to continue on with this mystery between the two famous navigators we find a report by the Frenchman Charles de la Ronciere who discovered a map in the National Library of Paris which he attributes to Columbu, that has a Latin inscription that describes the discovery of the Cape Verde Islands as having been made by Antonio da Noli.

So for the first time we have a document with arguments that show that Columbus had a direct interest in da Noli, which in fact is of tremendous importance for historians. This map is known as 'The Columbus Map'.

If this map was in fact made by Columbus, we can say logically that he would have wanted to meet da Noli to learn more about the sea and navigation. And when we follow the voyages of Columbus we are constantly following the voyages of da Noli.

In the town square in Noli (Italy) there are two plaques honoring the two navigators - Antonio da Noli and Christopher Columbus:

1. ANTONIO DA NOLI

He was fearless amongst the brave navigators of Noli

For half of the 15 th century

He discovered the Cape Verde Islands

Which opened up the route to India

By way of the Cape of Good Hope

The most fortunate foreigner

2. CHRISTOPHER COLUMBUS

21

On the 31st of May 1476, he came to Genoa with a fleet of 5 ships on the way to Holland. He left the port of Noli. This trip would prove to be decisive in his great destiny.

Being caught up in a sea battle, he was shipwrecked and took refuge in Portugal, where he settled and later went to Spain. His great navigational project was to unite the west with the east by crossing the Atlantic based on his strong Christian beliefs. His great courage and seamanship is unsurpassed, he discovered America, but more than anything he opened up navigation for other men to cross the oceans. His grand idea was made in an atmosphere of unity and peace amid the people of Noli.

Leo Magnini, an Italian historian describes some very important details about da Noli. He says that **this great Genoese navigator somehow never attained the glory earned by such great men as Magellan and Vasco da Gama, yet the West owes the expansion of western civilization in the far off lands of Africa, Asia and South America to him**.

He should also be better known on the Ligurian Coast (the Italian Riviera), his native land, and to which he always belonged. Magnini gives us a hypothetical argument made by the Portuguese author, Gaspar Ribeira Villas in which he theorizes that Antonio da Noli may have sailed from Cabo Verde to the coast of Brazil, either on his own initiative or as a suggestion from the Infante D. Henrique, thus justifying all the noteworthy benefits bestowed upon him, while enabling him to continue on with his expeditions and explorations.

This argument is very interesting because Villas also explains what was a curious fact registered in the year 1466 that had his brother Bartolomeu da Noli was named as the captain of the island of Santiago, so it appears that Antonio must have been away. Given the knowledge that the Noli family had complete control of the captaincy, one could suppose that Antonio could have sailed to the south, a task that would have been more to his temperament as a seaman.We can say that if this theory were to be true and if Columbus had spoken with him, he (Columbus) could have learned something about the southern part of the Atlantic Ocean and the possibility of finding new lands. This is especially so, since historians have often said that Columbus developed his ideas of getting to India by departing from Cabo Verde and going west (and if Antonio da Noli had actually sailed along the Brazilian coast he would have had to go south and also west). And it has already been shown that Columbus had several opportunities to come in direct contact with da Noli.

I know that most historians will not support such a thesis because it lacks historical facts. They might argue that if Antonio da Noli knew of a new continent the Portuguese would have extended the demarcation line in the Treaty of Alcacovas in 1479. Antonio da Noli had already been in Cabo Verde at this time for nearly 20 years and would have had plenty of time to discover a new continent (Brazil), but in reality we would have to analyze the times in which we are speaking:-

Portugal did not want to discover a new continent as much as it wanted to discover a new route to India, which was clearly the top priority.

Portugal would not have wanted to suggest that it knew of a secret continent, especially by demanding that the treaty be extended by 200 leagues, since all of these efforts would have been conducted in secrecy and all of their funds were being allocated for the trip to India.

But when Columbus returned from America with new information in 1492, Portugal also would have wanted a share in the glory, so in 1494 when they made the Treaty of Tordesilhas with Spain, they insisted that the line of demarcation be extended by two hundred leagues more than in the Treaty of Alcacovas (which was made in 1479). This gave the Portuguese the right to discover Brazil as we shall see later.

In 1499, at the end of the year, the Spanish explorer Pinzon made a trip to South America after departing from Cabo Verde and perhaps it was this voyage that brought attention for the 'official' discovery of Brazil by Pedro Alvares Cabral some three months later in 1500 (Cabral was already preparing for his trip to India).

So all of this information seems to be very logical because, after all, the Portuguese were very good navigators.

There is still another possibility, for example, during the years between 1476 and 1479 Antonio da Noli retained his position as captain of the island of Santiago during a period when Spain controlled Cabo Verde and before the Treaty of Alcacovas was signed. During this period he is seen as a traitor by some historians because he worked for the Spanish. But it is possible that he could have spoken with Columbus and convincing him that there was a new continent on the other side of the ocean, while not thinking too much about the consequences, because at this time his future would have been linked more to the fate of Spain than to that of Portugal. Columbus, after all was from the same country and he probably even knew Antonio's brother Agostinho, the map maker in Genoa.

The fact is, if one could prove a direct linkage between Antonio da Noli and Columbus, we could probably solve a lot of the mysteries about Columbus' life that has lasted for more than five centuries.

I am personally convinced that Columbus was in direct contact with da Noli. Why?

For me there are two outstanding facts for historians to examine: First, there is the map that was made around 1492 and attributed to Columbus and second, there is the map made by the petty officer Juan de la Cosa in 1500.

The first, because if Columbus did make this map, he had already indicated on the map itself that Antonio da Noli was the discoverer of Cabo Verde. So he had to know a lot about this navigator. Especially since Columbus had already been to Madeira and Cabo Verde between 1476 and 1485. During this time, Antonio da Noli was very much involved in the Atlantic trade with a profound interest in the sugar trade just like Columbus. Columbus, himself, was attracted to the Genoese communities in both Lisbon and Madeira and since there was also a Genoese community in Cabo Verde it would have been natural for him to spend some time amongst them (the genoese), taking into account Columbus' passion for learning as much as possible about navigation and the fact that the Genoese controlled much of the sugar trade.

The university history professor, Jose Luiz Comellas, from the University of Seville has also written a detailed report that examines the Columbus map and believes it to be an authentic work made by Columbus.

But what really convinced me was the discovery of the map made by Juan de las Cosas, the petty officer who sailed aboard the Santa Maria on Columbus' first voyage to America. This map was made in 1500 and bears many resemblances to the map attributed to Columbus but it clearly was not made by the same person. On this map there is an inscription that reads, 'Antonio's Island or Cabo Verde' alongside the Cape Verde Islands, so Columbus' petty officer confirms the fact that his crew was very much aware of Antonio's Island and or Cabo Verde because both maps, the one by Columbus and the other by his petty officer make references to Antonio da Noli.

In the Geographic Society of Lisbon there is a large facsimile of the Juan de las Cosas map and also a smaller reproduction of one that was found in the belongings of the famous Admiral and navigator, Gago Coutinho, who made the first airplane crossing of the South Atlantic route in a seaplane via Cabo Verde in 1922. He was also a well known Portuguese historian and cartographer.

Note: According to the Grande Encyclopedia Portuguesa Brasileira, Bartolomeu da Noli was the captain of the island of Santiago during a period in 1466 and when two priests, Frei Rogerio and Frei Jaime initiated an evangelization program on the islands, Bartolomeu da Noli led a scandalous life. Because of the intervention of Frei Rogerio, his lover abandoned him, so Bartolomeu ordered his assassination (Frei Roger) and Frei Jaime was blamed for the murder and imprisoned. Fearing a popular uprising from the Cape Verdean inhabitants, the priest was released.

Now we can pretty much agree with Leo Magnini that Antonio da Noli was in fact the 'official' discoverer of Cabo Verde and is considered as one of the most important Portuguese navigators of the 15th century as new revelations and documents can easily verify this history. Another very important detail is the fact that these islands are never mentioned in Portuguese documents before the year 1460 and curiously all the other navigators who claim to be the discoverer, always give dates before 1460. Magnini recognizes the genius of Portugal's collaboration with Genoa and using their experience at sea and commerce, which was undoubtedly one of the major factors in Portugal's overseas expansion.

And we must recognize that ironically, Antonio da Noli was a Genoese, a Portuguese as well as being the first Cape Verdean and founder of the old capital of Santiago-Ribeira Grande, as the first European city below the tropical zone (the islands were uninhabited when discovered).

Unfortunately this history faces many arguments, both positive and negative. For example when we take a closer look at this history, in spite of all the great achievements of these navigators in navigation, science, geography, cartography, commerce, etc. We always come across the atrocities of slavery and the mentality of the Europeans with their ideas of Western civilization. The Europeans unfortunately give great names to these episodes such as the Renaissance or the Age of Discoveries. We cannot forget the blood letting of these civilizations and for these reasons I believe that we now have a golden opportunity to create a new Era of Reconciliation. In this way we can recognize both the great achievements of the great navigators such as Antonio da Noli, Vasco da Gama and Columbus, while at the same time we can recognize their great atrocities (if any). We always say that they were great men of courage, a fact that we must accept without much doubt because this is apparently true.

But if we really want to commemorate their greatness, we should practice a little of their courage. And the best way to demonstrate this courage would be to reveal the truth and officially recognize both the positive and the negative.

This argument can be very valuable especially at this point in history, since we are already in 1997 and this is the 500th anniversary of the death of Antonio da Noli as well as Vasco da Gama's voyage to India. Ironically Expo 98 is to celebrate the return of Vasco da Gama to Lisbon in 1498 (made possible by da Noli) but now there are only a few people who understand the connection between these two navigators and their great discoveries. If we have the will and the courage to

26

acknowledge this history we can then tie it directly to the Age of Reconciliation as we approach the next millennium in the year 2000 when we will also be commemorating another famous navigator, Pedro Alvares Cabral and the discovery of Brazil in 1500, who, like Vasco da Gama, also owes his fame to Antonio da Noli and Cabo Verde. It would be a great shame if we do not take full advantage of this opportunity.

We now understand a great deal about the history of Cabo Verde and slavery, the achievements and the atrocities and with this experience, it can be seen as a model for the next 500 years.

For example we can establish direct contacts with various cities around the world to create sister city programs, that have Cape Verdean roots, such as Portuguese; Cape Verdeans - Italians; Cape Verdeans - Angolans; Cape Verdeans - Americans; Cape Verdeans etc., to demonstrate our will to reconcile this history with the goal of improving relations amongst the different cultures that were directly affected by this historical experience.

Eventually this philosophy can be expanded to other countries.

And finally, to confirm the importance of Antonio da Noli and his role in history we can analyze his achievements:

1. He opened the way for the discovery of Brazil and the discovery of a sea route to India. This fact is usually lost in history because most people are unaware of the historical role enjoyed by Cabo Verde. However these islands served the Portuguese kingdom with tremendous benefits.

2. A logistical base was established on the islands that would provide ships with supplies, provisions, repairs, manual labor etc.

3. Geographically the discovery of the islands served as an excellent substitute for the aspirations of the Portuguese kings who had often attempted to control the Canary Islands in their constant wars with Spain. Now with the occupation of Cabo Verde, Portugal could leave the Canary Islands to Spain without any problems, because geographically and strategically the control of the archipelago of Cabo Verde had an extraordinary importance to the Portuguese in their quest for overseas

expansion and control of the seas. So Portugal was able to forfeit any claims to the Canary Islands in the treaties of Alcacovas and Tordesilhas in favor of Spain.

4. With the control of these islands Portugal could control the African coastal trade very economical, because it was much easier to guard the African coast from a centralized sea base than it would have been to fund military operations in African seaports to control the Atlantic Ocean and protect the administrators.

5. Cabo Verde served as a major trading station with America, Europe, Africa and Asia and demonstrated an incredible will for a country as small as Portugal. For the first time it was involved in international trade on a major level, which lasted for more than two centuries, as well as control of the great oceans of the world.

6. Antonio da Noli was instrumental in helping Portugal develop relations with Genoa especially in commerce, while attracting many highly skilled Genoese to Portugal during the period of overseas expansion.

7. The Catholic church was established in Cabo Verde and this was the first time that Christianity was established outside of the Old World and the Middle East and eventually it became a launching pad for Christianity in Africa, America and Asia.

8. Cabo Verde served as an experimental laboratory for new planting systems such as cotton, sugar cane, coffee, tobacco and the raising of horses and livestock etc.

9. Cabo Verde served as a secret navigational school for navigators and the conquest and expansion of the oceans. Many historians believe that da Noli was an important factor during these explortions and probably helped Dias and da Gama in the preparation for their trip to India.

10. Cabo Verde served as the historical central point for the transfer of old world values to the New World. Many animals and plants were introduced to the New World by cape verdeans. Likewise many were introduced to the Old World by Cape Verdeans.

11. The cotton plantation system was copied by the Americans and served as a base for the American economy for many years. Many historians believe that it was this plantation system that became a key issue in the breakout of the American civil war which clearly transformed American society and the history of the world.

12. Cabo Verde also served as a central point for introducing Africans to the New World and to Europe which undoubtedly served as a major base for the creation of a new society shared between hispanics and lusophones in these countries which resulted in a new mestizo race with tremendous influence in the American countries, especially since the Africans were highly skilled in agricultural technology in tropical countries such as Brazil, Cuba, Puerto Rico etc.

13. Cabo Verde also served as a base for the first non-European navigators to sail their own boats across the Atlantic with immigrants and merchandise to American countries on a regular schedule (the schooner - Ernestina with Captain Henry Mendes at the helm with at least 55 Atlantic crossings is an excellent example).

14. Cabo Verde became the first society to organize an international trade program for the continents of Africa, America, Europe, Asia and Australia.

15. Cabo Verde served as a key point to control the African coast from Morocco in the north to Liberia in the south, along the west coast of Africa.

16. And obviously the slave trade had a dramatic impact on the African continent. Horses were also exported to Africa from Cabo Verde.

17. Cabo Verde was the central point in the Treaty of Tordesilhas which divided the world into two great societies with the result that now 300 million people are Spanish speaking and 200 million are Portuguese speaking.
18. The creation of the Creole language. The world's first Creole language is believed to have been created here in Cabo Verde.

19. The creation of new musical sounds which have an influence from many nations but offers a special blend that makes it uniquely cape verdean. A major part of African and Latin music has Cape Verdean influences while cape verdean sounds have also been influenced directly from these countries as well as European nations, especially Poland and Portugal.

20. Cabo Verde served as a crucial stop for Magellan's crew which proved that the world was round. It was here, in 1522, that Sebastion del Cano (an officer of Magellan's crew) confirmed that the world was round.

21. Cabo Verde became a central point in the study of geography, science, aviation, navigation, astronomy, agriculture, anthropology etc.

22. Portugal was able to control large and small countries on five continents for five centuries while influencing the historical destinies of at least 30 other nations.

23. The establishment of an Iberian culture in the Americas, Africa and Asia.

24. And the Treaty of Tordesilhas may well be the most important treaty in the history of the world when we examine the details therein.

25. And so Cabo Verde is well positioned today to offer leadership on the eve of the next millennium with the possibility of offering solutions to the many racial problems that exist throughout the world.

We shouldn't forget that many of the celebrations of the 500th anniversary of the discoveries is for the winners, those who in reality were responsible for enslaving a large segment of Indian and African societies with incredible repercussions from which they still suffer today. So it is very important for the world to reflect upon their past mistakes and look forward to a new era in the history of mankind, with the understanding that we must learn to share this planet with all of humanity. So especially following the commemorations of Expo - 98 we would like to be able demonstrate our will to fight for equality and not for the continuation of inequality for the next millennium.

Now the historians can begin to revise Cape Verdean history with the aim of explaining it without preconceptions and show the world how a determined people can manage to survive in today's world with very limited natural resources. And certainly how the discovery of this archipelago had a major impact on the world community in many aspects and really changed the history of mankind, especially with such navigators as Columbus, Vasco da Gama, Cabral and Magellan. All of these men received direct assistance from Cape Verdeans which made it possible for their names to be engraved indelibly in the history of mankind.

We must not forget the achievements of the famous Portuguese pilots Gago Coutinho and Sacadura Cabral and the American Charles Lindbergh and the famous writers Herman Melville and Charles Darwin, all of whom were directly influenced by assistance directly from Cabo Verde. We should also remember the great Cape Verdean writers and the movement known as Claridade (enlightenment) in the middle of the 20th century, such as Baltasar Lopes, Jorge Barbosa, Pedro Cardosa and Manuel Lopes amongst many others. Then, of course , there is Amilcar Cabral one of the great leaders in the independence movement for the African countries and one of Cabo Verde's most honored sons.

Thus, we see that Cabo Verde has been a major influence on humanity and a major participant in her role in the center of the transformation of this history. Without any preconceptions of history it can be agreed that documentation exists regarding the influence of Antonio da Noli in this history and his impact on the discovery period. According to

31

the historian Luis Albuquerque 'the discovery of the Cape Verde Islands and with the establishment of a logistical base in the city of Ribeira Grande on the Island of Santiago and the establishment of a Portuguese port in this area, the role of the Archipelago of the Canary Islands lost its value and the Portuguese would forfeit their claims to it."

In exchange, D. Afonso V and his son got a promise of non-intervention from the Spanish;for their discoveries and commerce along the coast of Africa;, from the southern point of this archipelago, that which was without any doubt whatsoever of extraordinary importance ".(Ref: Albuquerque's comments on the compromises established by the Treaty of Alcacovas (1479).

We can also provide more conformation of the importance of da Noli by reading the words of Leo Magnini - "There is no doubt that Antonio da Noli provided very important services, which were not just limited to the discovery of the Cape Verde Islands for the Portuguese crown. He, in fact, opened the route of discovery for Brazil as well as a new route to India "

(Ref: Antonio da Noli and the Collaboration between the Portuguese and the Genoese in the Maritime Discoveries, July 1962 p-6).

Notes"(Ref: Historia Geral de Cabo Verde - Corpo Documental Vol. 1 1988 - Documentos No. 2,3, & 38)

1. The names Santiago and Sal were known as Sam Jacobo and Lana in a royal letter of 3 December 1460 where we find the names of the Cape Verde Islands mentioned for the first time, but here there isn't any mention of the discoveries or the discoverers. It seems that between the two royal letters of 3 December 1460 and that of 19 September 1462, there were five islands discovered during the life of the Infante D. Henrique in 1460 and the others between 1461 and 1462. There are those who believe that the last group of islands were discovered by the navigator- scribe Diogo Afonso who was sent to the archipelago to confirm the number of islands that were in the area. This is an important argument because this navigator was awarded a captaincy for the northern part of the island of Santiago while da Noli was awarded the captaincy for the southern part of the same island, where he personally founded

the capital - Ribeira Grande which is now called Cidade Velha and its ruins are a tourist attraction today. *(Ref: Carta das Ilhas de Cabo Verde de Valentim Fernandes 1506 e 1508 por A.F. Fontana da Costa, Lisboa 1939, Divisao de Publicacoes e Biblioteca Agencia Geral das Colonias 1939).*
Fortunately I found this book in the Biblioteca da Ajuda de Lisboa (BAL) and according to the information in this book; **"Diogo Afonso, the scribe of the Infante D. Henrique, was the fortunate discoverer of the remaining islands of Cabo Verde and his name is not involved in any controversy whatsoever."**
The names of these islands are seen for the first time in the letter of 19 Sep. 1462 - Brava, Sao Nicolau, Sao Vicente, Raso and Branco, Santa Luzia and Santo Antao, without indicating who discovered them, but this was resolved shortly thereafter with the verification that it was in fact - Diogo Afonso, who was named in a new royal letter of 29 Oct. 1462**. The author of this book made an interesting analysis about the discovery of the first five islands and made the same conclusion that I did, and that being that da Noli was the Official discoverer of Cabo Verde.

 * *Alguns Documentos da Torre do Tombo serie vermelha No. 3495 p-31and 32.*
 ** *Alguns Documentos da Torre do Tombo serie vermelha No. 3495 p-32.*

After the death of da Noli in 1497 the endowment was transferred to his daughter in a royal letter by D. Manuel dated 8 April 1497 with the rights of the captaincy which would be transferred to D. Branca de Aguiar - the daughter of Antonio da Noli with the condition that they would be managed by her future husband who would be selected by the king because there were not any male heirs. According to an Italian encyclopedia Antonio da Noli married a Portuguese woman from the family of Aguiar.

An important statement made in this letter states;
"According to our information as we have it, Mr. Antonio da Noli was the first to discover this island (Santiago)."

This declaration is written testimony that da Noli discovered Santiago and by implication the other four islands that were mentioned as well.

2. Ref: Columbus and the Portuguese Voyages - F. Caraci 1988 - p-5.

• Some historians believe that Columbus lived in Portugal between the years 1478 and 1485 (Ref: Ferro G. La Navigazioni Lusitana nell'Atlantico e Cristavao Columbo in Portugallo, Milano, 1984 pp 221-245).

Normally in Portugal itself, the Portuguese say he was there between 1476 and 1485. But they also believe that during his stay in Portugal that he spent time in Cabo Verde and on the coast of Guine as well as in Madeira and the Azores as cited in this reference.

3. Ref: Notizie Storiche su Noli: Ciclo di Studi e Ricerche di Palazzo del Comune Noli 1982.

4. Ref: Le Historie della Vita e dei Fatti di Cristoforo Colombo per D. Fernando, suo figlio. Vol - 1 - Edizioni "Alpes", Milano

CABO VERDE AND BRAZIL

The Historical Ties

To understand the relationship between Cabo Verde and Brazil we must start with the Treaty of Tordesilhas in 1494. The foundation for the discovery and control of Brazil began with this treaty when Cabo Verde served as the pinnacle of the treaty because of the key geographical and strategic position that she occupied. During this era it was very difficult to know the strategic points in the sea outside of the Atlantic Islands. So to facilitate the treaty process, the Iberian countries, Spain and Portugal decided to promote Cabo Verde as the principal point. Since it was well known by navigators and the rest of the sea was unknown, Cabo Verde became like a beacon in the middle of the ocean that would be the basis for dividing the world in two strategic parts, one half for Spain and the other half for Portugal vis-a-vis the new discoveries that would be carried out by these two countries.

In this sense the navigator Pedro Alvares Cabral arrived in Cabo Verde in 1500 in a voyage that has been historically fraught with controversy about his true intentions, because he did have instructions to sail to India by way of Cabo Verde. But on the way to India while arriving in Cabo Verde, is when the controversy usually begins. Some writers believe that he had a secret mandate to discover Brazil, because it seems that the Portuguese already had an idea that there might be a new continent there (this was probably due to the influence of the voyage made by Columbus in 1492) and so he could make his final plans to discover the new land (Brazil), once he arrived in Cabo Verde.

There are other writers who say that he arrived in Brazil after being caught in a storm and was blown off course. In any case there is a document containing instructions to go to Cabo Verde on his route to India. The fact is that he did discover Brazil on this trip and he did send a ship back to Portugal to confirm it with the Portuguese authorities as he took his fleet of ships to India. This is a very important fact for the history of Brazil because the Spanish were also at sea making new discoveries and there are those authors who believe that a Spanish navigator - Pinzon had anchored on the Brazilian coast a few months before Cabral. However, as Cabral was able to confirm his discovery first, Brazil was awarded to Portugal, especially because the demarcation zone was in favor of Portugal, thanks to the geographical position of Cabo Verde in the Treaty of Tordesilhas.

In the 16th century, the archipelago of Cabo Verde became a preferential stopping off point for supplies and repairs for ships crossing the Atlantic on the way to India, the African coast, the islands in the Gulf of Guine (Bijagos) and to Brazil.

The supplies and aid for the first Brazilian settlers, consisted of the transfer of food bearing plants, domestic animals, livestock and horses from the old world to the new world.

Wheat in particular, had to be shipped to Brazil via Cabo Verde. Later when plants and animals started to reproduce themselves in the new world, the process became self perpetuating.

The islands of Sao Nicolau and Santa Luzia provided an excellent supply of fish, and ships would stop to fish on their routes to Brazil and Sao Tome.

It was common practice for ships to anchor at Cabo Verde to solve many of their problems when they were crossing the Atlantic. Due to her geographical position in the middle of the ocean amid various continents, Cabo Verde became a necessary stopping place for repairs and supplies for the Portuguese armed forces, especially during the first decades of the 16th century. Besides this, Cabo Verde was obligated to provide supplies and assistance to ships of the Portuguese kingdom.

According to a letter between Antonio Correia from the Ribeira Grande Town Hall (Santiago) and the Secretary of the Kingdom, dated 25 Oct. 1512, the port of Ribeira Grande was very important for the commerce of ships heading for Sao Tome and Principe, Mina, Brazil and all along the coast of Guine.

At the end of the 19th century, Cape Verdeans provided plenty of assistance to passenger ships with European emigrants coming from Germany, England and Italy and relocating to Brazil, South Africa and Australia. The steam

ships had to stop for refueling (coal), food supplies, repairs and recreation at Porto Grande in Mindelo, Sao Vicente. All of this information is documented with the names of the shipping companies and their destinations between 1887 and 1890. There are many traditions on the island of Santo Antao and those of the Creoles in Rio Grande do Norte in Brazil which are almost identical. Clearly the cape verdeans had to have shipped many slaves to the coast of Brazil.

In the 20th century, in the year 1922, the first south Atlantic flight was made between Portugal and Brazil, and the pilots were obligated to make a two week stop-over in Cabo Verde between the 5th and 16th of April. A notable fact is that this stop-over between Cabo Verde and Brazil would be the last flight for the famous seaplane, the Lusitania.

Then in 1939 the Italians built an airport on the island of Sal. After building the airport, the Italians used it to transport Italians to Brazil and apparently to other destinations such as Argentina and Uruguay with assistance from Cape Verdeans with their stop-overs in Sal.

There are also many relations between the music and literature and other cultural aspects of Cabo Verde with those of Brazil. And Brazil, despite being on the other side of the Atlantic seems to be omnipresent throughout history, in Cape Verdean literature and music.

Once the catholic church established a foothold in Cabo Verde and the new world, many slaves were baptized as Christians and brought their new religion with them to Brazil.

Another important fact in the connection between Brazil and Cabo Verde is the type of passengers we find going from Portugal to Brazil. Of course, there are many relations between slaves in Brazil and the archipelago of Cabo Verde, but there were also other passengers. These passengers were forced to go as condemned to exile in Angola and Brazil.

There were also many merchants from Portugal and Spain traveling to Brazil in search of riches they hoped to find in this new land.

And in the second half of the 16th century and the beginning of the 17th century almost all the commerce on the west African coast going to the new world was shipped through Santiago. The city of Ribeira Grande was in this endeavor a compulsory port of call. It was from there that 'slaves and other African merchandise' would be shipped to Brazil and the Antilles.

Another important detail about the slaves is the fact that many of them came from Angola and shipped to Brazil by way of Cabo Verde. These Africans reportedly applied better tropical agricultural techniques than the European colonizers.

In the book 'Cabo Verde os Bastidores da Independencia' 1996, the author Jose Vicente Lopes tells us that in the second decade of the 19th century Cabo Verde made its first attempt to separate itself from Portugal.

On the island of Santiago there was a Cape Verdean movement to unite with Brazil, following the Liberal Revolution in Portugal of 24 Aug. 1820.

Brazil proclaimed her independence on 7 September 1822, but Lopes explains that according to the historian Daniel A. Pereira, the idea did not materialize because of a lack of maturity for the movement and the non-existence of a middle class strong enough to support it as well as intellectuals and conscientious citizens capable of circulating and planting new ideas for the future. But in any case it would have been extremely difficult to carry out and virtually impossible, because of the Treaty of Recognition between Portugal and Brazil which was mediated by England and signed on the 29 Aug. 1825. This treaty would become an impediment regarding the Portuguese colonies and relations with Brazil. Article No. 3 of this treaty states 'Your Imperial Majesty promises not to accept any kind of proposals from any of the Portuguese colonies that want to meet with Brazil'.

Obviously Cabo Verde played a major role in the development in the beginning of this country as well as in the 19th and 20th centuries.

There have been several new articles published in Portugal regarding new developments in the discovery of Brazil. New information indicates a strong possibility that it was Pacheco Duarte Pereira who was the first to arrive in Brazil about 18 months prior to Pedro Alvares Cabral.

This argument has strong supporters from France, Portugal and Spain, because they cooperated on a special research project to determine the truth of this important discovery. One article in particular attributed to a new magazine "Super

Interessante" that was published for the first time in Portugal with a dateof May 1998, reveals that Cabral was ordered to take possession of Brazil in 1500 because Portugal was definitely aware of its existence. His other major mission was to establish a trading post in India.

The reason given for this order by Portugal was that Cabral was a member of the Order of Christ, and that only a member of this organization was legally entitled to take possession of new lands. The Ordem do Cristo (The Order of Christ) was a religious military organization, autonomous to the state and the successor to the mysterious Ordem dos Templarios (Order of the Templars) which had special authorization from the Pope, to occupy and take possession of territories taken from the infidels, as was done during the Christian Crusades (In this case land taken from the indians in Brazil).

On 26 April 1500, 4 days after he spotted the Brazilian coastline, Cabral raised the flag of the Order of Christ and had the first mass conducted in the new territory, in a location that is now called Porto Seguro. This religious ceremony sponsored by the Order of Christ, gave Portugal formal authority over the new possession. It would be this organization (The Order Of Christ) that would eventually transform a small European nation into an imperial power spread across the four corners of the globe. This is very interesting information of course, but as we shall see though out the pages of this book, the secret ingredient to making this system work, was understanding the importance of the discovery of Cabo Verde and maximizing the potential of these islands along with the new settlers (the Cape Verdean people).

I would like to close this report on Brazil with some personal observations regarding slavery throughout history. I find that there are few historical details on this subject , for example:

1. Normally there isn't much said about the type of person who became a slave. Very often we find that these slaves were knowledgeable in agriculture, leadership and other skills. That is because they weren't necessarily slaves before they were captured. This feature of slavery had tremendous value for tropical countries such as Brazil, because these slaves were accustomed to tropical climates.

2. Normally nothing is said about the suffering that they endured on the slave ships, but certainly many of them died on these routes, because the conditions could be extremely painful, with lack of personal hygiene and little space for moving their bodies.

3. The church doesn't' say much about slavery, but the truth is it was very much involved in this trade. **In fact in Cabo Verde the church maintained slaves as church property.** We now have a report about a problem involving the Portuguese kingdom and the church regarding a deceased bishop, D. Pedro Brandao and his estate in Cabo Verde. He died in 1607 and the New Bishop D. Luis Pereira de Miranda of Cabo Verde made a claim on his estate, because, after all, he was the successor and believed that he should inherit the goods because they belonged to the Church. This case is very interesting because it shows the church's point of view regarding slavery, since there were slaves as part of the estate. According to the author Nuno da Silva Goncalves, we have new revelations about this problem in a book that has been recently published and based on documents found in the Secret Archives of the Vatican and the Vatican Apostalic Library in addition to documentation discovered at the Biblioteca da Ajuda in Lisbon. In any case the Vatican expressed a deep interest in this problem with the hope that the authorities would be able to solve it while protecting the image of the church. In this particular case the slaves were awarded to the Bishop D. Luis Pereira de Miranda, along with other goods, in a letter dated 28 January 1610.

4. And to understand the mentality of a slave trader, I remember the story about an African trader who celebrated the sale of his slaves with the European buyer and after getting drunk with whiskey, the buyer had him shipped out with the rest of the slaves.

CABO VERDE THE NUCLEUS OF THE HISPANIC AND LUSOPHONE SOCIETIES

This report is based on the concept that Cabo Verde was the central point in the beginning of the new world and had a major impact during the creation of a new society in one of the most important phases in the history of mankind - the Age of Discoveries. In this case I am speaking of the direct and indirect influences of Cabo Verde within the Spanish and African societies which resulted in a new Hispanic society (and also Lusophone). The majority of historians have been unable to bring this history together because the historical links were missing.

However, with more interest on the history of the discoveries and Expo-98, writers are beginning to investigate this subject. Personally, I know of a history professor of a major American university who was born and raised in Cuba, but had no idea how Africans arrived in this country. Until now this subject has not been taught in schools. But in any case it is a very important subject that must be taken into account if we want to understand the complexity of the history of mankind and the problems that go with it. For this reason, I'm hoping to be able to demonstrate that this is truly a fascinating subject worth studying.

Unfortunately we must understand that there are many people who lost their historic roots during this famous period of the discoveries. So, I believe that it is very important to explain a little of this history which is generally unknown to the world.

First of all we would like to examine some of the effects on the world with the discovery of the Cape Verde Islands. This discovery unfortunately would be a major base for the slave trade under the jurisdiction of the Portuguese. Cabo Verde itself was founded in 1460 by the Portuguese. The islands were uninhabited at this time (according to most historians) and the Portuguese began to settle there in 1462. During this period Portugal was exploring the African coast line and were dealing in the slave trade, especially on the coast of Guine. Therefore,

41

because of Cabo Verde's geographical position in the Atlantic Ocean and 500 kilometers off the coast of Africa, it would assume a major influential role in the slave trade. Here on these islands, many slaves arrived in Portuguese ships to populate the uninhabited islands, while supplying manual labor during the creation of a new society with an enormous impact on the world.

There were also Arab prisoners; who were captured during the wars with the Muslims in Morocco; who were among the first settlers of Cabo Verde.

These islands always had a stormy history during the creation and expansion of two great societies, the Hispanics on one side and the Lusophones on the other. We can say that it was here, without any doubt, that birth was given to these historical societies in the New World. Because it was here where we find a lot of influence from the catholic churches of Spain and Portugal right from the beginning of the creation of Cabo Verde. To prove this argument we simply ask you to go to the islands of Fogo and Santiago and see the chapels that were built by the Spanish, with their historical elements still there to verify it.

Besides this, there was a lot of commerce on the African coastline conducted with Cabo Verde, Portugal and Spain. Historically the Spanish were in the center of this trade with many residents living in Ribeira Grande, the commerce center on the island of Santiago. Of course there is a lot of history in this area that needs to be studied, but this book is mainly to review the main points. In this way we can build a foundation to examine this subject in greater detail.

So let us begin:

1. The discovery of Cabo Verde in 1460 had a major impact on the development of the slave trade in the rivers of Guine along the African coast.

2. This trade was well known in Portugal and Spain and attracted the Spanish as much as the Portuguese, Italians and Jews (new Christians) to the archipelago. And it would be these groups that would make up the majority of the white race in Cabo Verde during this period.

3. But exactly when did the Spanish start to come to Cabo Verde? The first significant group of foreign residents on the islands of Cabo Verde, whether being permanent residents or temporary inhabitants, were the Spanish. One of the first chapels on these islands was established by the Spanish. We can find historical artifacts relating to these chapels in Santiago and Fogo that can be traced back to the 15th century.

In 1466 we find references made to the first Spaniards to reside in Cabo Verde. These were two Franciscan monks, Frei Rogerio and Frei Jaime, from the convent of St. Bernadino de Atouguia (Spain) and provided religious assistance to Antonio da Noli, the captain of Ribeira Grande.

The Spanish also occupied Cabo Verde between 1477 and 1479. Despite, seizing control of the islands from the Portuguese during this period, the King of Spain allowed Antonio da Noli to continue to govern the islands. But it seems that it would have been after Columbus' second voyage to America, when the Spanish really began to establish themselves on the islands. Following the discovery of the Antilles islands and the rest of the American continent, there was a lot of commercial trade development being conducted with the inhabitants of Santiago. The main objective of this commerce was to provide the necessary manual labor for the settlers of the Indias de Castela (the name given to the West Indies by the Spanish).

Indias de Castela was the name that was applied to the islands and the lands of Central America that were being discovered and explored by the Spanish. This name was given because Columbus thought that he had actually discovered India and had arrived in the Far East, so this area became known as Indias de Castela or Indias Ocidentais (West Indies).

At first when the European population established themselves in these territories, they had tried to use the local indigenous inhabitants for the more strenuous work, but unfortunately, this experience did not have any positive results, in fact it led to the decimation of the local Indian groups. Trying to satisfy the greedy appetite for quick enrichment, the Spanish demanded that the Indians expend more energy that it was their natural capacity to produce. So being unable to meet these stringent standards the Indians preferred to flee or commit suicide.

This awkward attempt to get the Indians to do the hard labor for the exploration of the new territories, along with the fact that there was a rising movement to defend the civil rights of the Indians by several groups, were be two conditions that favored the increase of African slaves being imported to the islands of the New World.

Bartelemeu de las Casas was one of the major defenders of the civil rights of the Indians. This priest went to America in 1562 where he observed first hand, for eight years the situation regarding the treatment of the labor force by the settlers in the New World. Having had this experience he returned to Spain where he defended the liberty of the Indians. He was named by Cardinal Asneros as the universal magistrate and protector of the Indians, as it was declared that there would not be any reason, be it war , rebellion or redemption, that would allow the Indians to be enslaved.

In effect, slavery was perfectly acceptable to the Christian monarchies, particularly by those of the Iberians, especially when taking 'infidel' prisoners in the Muslim wars or blacks purchased in different areas along the African coast.

Thus it was from 1501 that the catholic kings authorized the exportation of black slaves to leave the Spanish ports for the West Indies to replace the Indian labor force.

They had a pressing need to find supply points to provide African slaves. Up until the end of the 15th century Lisbon was the place where the Spanish businessmen purchased their slaves. Beginning in the 16th century, many of these merchants started to buy them directly from the provisional port of Santiago in Cabo Verde. It was cheaper for them to purchase the slaves this way, than in Lisbon. Once the slaves were off loaded in Spain they would be re-exported to the West Indies by ships that specialized in these routes under the name Carreira das Indias (the Route to India).

According to certain Spanish historians, namely Ricardo Grego Martinez, this route became firmly established after Columbus' second voyage to the Indias de Castela. So now we can analyze the commercial effect of slaves on Hispanic culture. At first we can clearly thank the defenders of the Indian's civil rights and the religious leaders such as Bartelemeu de las Casas and Cardinal Asneros along with the general conscience of the catholic kings and the Pope who didn't oppose the institution of slavery. African slaves were exported through Cabo Verde to the New World (Castela das Indias) at the beginning of the 16th century. But apparently the Spanish were already buying slaves in Lisbon before this. Unfortunately, it is a little difficult to verify much of this slave history in the 16th century, especially in Spain. I believe that it is possible to find this information in the Palacio de las Indias in Seville.

At any rate we already know that the African slaves made a tremendous impact on the Spanish slave routes to Castela de las Indias, which resulted in safeguarding to some extent some of the Indian culture in America, by providing substitute labor, albeit slave labor as the case was. Fortunately there are many documents confirming the names of ships and Spaniards who were involved in this trade. This business was conducted directly on the islands of Cabo Verde where the slaves were purchased, usually on the island of Santiago and the documents are located in the National Archives of the Torre do Tombo in Lisbon.

Now we should try to understand some of the conditions of the Treaty of Tordesilhas. This treaty prohibited the entry of Spanish ships along the African coast below the Canary Islands and they (the Spanish) could not participate in any commerce in those areas controlled by the Portuguese. Yet in truth there weren't any real impediments to the Spanish who were very adept at getting around the treaty. They simply moved to Cabo Verde and purchased the slaves there, since there were no laws against that practice, so were able to conduct business as usual. They became very well established and accepted in Santiago. The Portuguese liked them because they could import better agricultural produce from Spain for consumption by the islanders. According to one contemporary anonymous writer during this period in the middle of the 16th

45

century, "I saw many nice homes firmly fixed and inhabited by Portuguese and Spanish gentlemen in an area containing more than five hundred homes."

Another form of Spanish involvement was by forming partnerships with resident ship owners in commercial activities that were being developed in the region, while making up the greater part of the crew that would go there, then wait for the ship to get back to Cabo Verde and then claim control of their business dealings.

Hence, the Spanish played a significant role in the slave trade while based in Cabo Verde, with direct implications for the American continents.

The non-native foreign population on Cabo Verdeconsisted mainly of the resident Spanish, whether they were full time residents or temporary workers. Given that most of these were directly or indirectly involved in commerce, people of European origins were concentrated in Ribeira Grande, the main commercial center on the archipelago where most business was conducted.

Another important phase of the connection between the Lusophone and Hispanic societies was the lack of attractions for European women to reside on the islands. The absence of European women led to a new society of mestizos. Nothing prevented the Europeans from having relations with their slaves, even noblemen maintained intimate relations with their black slaves or mestizo women and any children that would be born as a result of this mixture would be legally and morally recognized (and many of them became lanzados or slave traders) and dealt with the slave trade in Africa. This was advantageous because they usually spoke African dialects as well as European languages.

To understand some of the activities involving Spain, Portugal and Cabo Verde and the beginning of slavery, there are some details that the reader should study.

The Spanish purchased their slaves on the islands of Cabo Verde and shipped them to Seville at first, then later they shipped them to the Antilles (West Indies in the Caribbean).

They also did this in Portugal. One example of this practice was accomplished by a businessman in Alfama (Portugal), Leonardo da Silveira, who in 1583 sent his ship 'Nossa Senhora do Cabo' to Cape Verdean contractors in Cabo Verde. The ship was sent from Lisbon to the island of Santiago to load units of slaves (pecas de escravos) and to transport them to Seville. Here we should understand that it was common practice when conducting business between the Portuguese and the Spanish to make contracts while forming partnerships. In effect this practice would become a major expansion of the slave trade as the New World adventurers and businessmen would always order more slaves to profit in this area.

The Spanish all over the New World were making new conquests and discoveries of huge territories in South and North America in countries such as Peru, Haiti, the Dominican Republic, Mexico, New Spain, Puerto Rico, Jamaica etc. **Initially the island of Santo Domingos (The Dominican Republic) was the main destination port for the African slaves.**

Later other ports would receive them. These new routes would be in Antilles, Cuba, Puerto Rico, La Hispanhola (Haiti and the Dominican Republic) and other small nucleuses like Trinidad, Marguerita and the Gulf of Venezuela. The large ports of this trade were in Havana, Cartagena, Nombre de Dios, Portobelo and San Juan.

Santo Domingos received a large number of Africans; and served as the commercial receiving area; that were being supplied from Santiago, Cabo Verde, which was the nucleus of this trade.

It was said that this island Santo Domingos (Hispaniola) was, the spring-board that produced 'the great leap forward' in the direction of the new territories, the logistical base for the Spanish conquest of the American continent and its people, in a constant search for gold, this was the 'human nourishment' for this task.

From the middle of the decade of 1520 the Spanish monarchy authorized diverse residents of Santo Domingos to introduce African slaves purchased in Cabo Verde, to help them in their work to explore this island (Hispaniola).

We must also remember that **Cabo Verde was a part of Spain between 1580 and 1640** (but as we noted earlier, **Spain also occupied and controlled Cabo Verde between 1477 and 1479**).

According to Charles Verlinden, in his book 'Antonio da Noli and the Colonization of the Cape Verde Islands' 1963, in 1476 a Spanish expedition attacked Santiago. On the 28th of March 1476, Anton Martin Neto received orders to arm ships to overtake any possessions of their Portuguese adversary, especially Antonio's (da Noli) Island otherwise known as the island of Santiago. The Spanish made contact with Antonio da Noli and the King D. Fernando ended up placing him under the protection of the Spanish crown while allowing him to continue to govern the island. This was somewhat interesting if not incredible, because the Spanish commander of the expedition Anton Martin Neto had already been promised the captaincy as a reward for his successful mission and now Antonio da Noli would continue to govern the island as he had for the previous fifteen years. Here we find an amazing demonstration of the talents and importance of Antonio da Noli as a negotiator, because not only did he continue to govern the island for Spain, (his adversary) but years later when Portugal regained control of the islands with the Treaty of Alcacovas, he still continued to govern the islands again for Portugal. This information was clearly written in a mandate by the King D. Fernando dated 6 Jun. 1477.

This document is very important in the history of Cabo Verde and Antonio do Noli, so I am including the whole document because it clearly establishes the direct links between the birth of the Hispanic society and Cabo Verde BEFORE Columbus made his first voyage to America, as well as being the nucleus of the Lusophone society.

It reads:

Don Fernando, by the grace of God, the king of Castille, of Leon etc. and to my great Admiral of the ocean and to my great justice of Castille and to the Infantes, Earles, Dukes, Counts , Marquises, rich men, masters of the Orders, and mayors of Castille, bankers, councilors, judges, gentlemen, scribes, officials, men of good standing and all the citizens of the towns and cities and all the lands and estates within my kingdom, and to all my great captains of the ocean and their men, and to any other captains, lords and masters and military personnel who participate in any type of armada or any other means by way of the oceans, ports and works of my kingdom and estates, as well as in any other locations, those who are my vassals and natural subjects, and to each and everyone of you, to whom this letter is to be shown or otherwise brought to public attention. Let it be known that I have taken for me and in behalf of the most serene queen, my loving wife, and for our royal crown, the island of Cabo Verde, and that the captain Mr. Antonio da Noli, a Genoese; and my gift and will is for her and those close to her as well as her advisors and that the cited Mr. Antonio da Noli will be known by the vassals and lands of my royal crown, and that those of you who are my subjects, will not in any way bring any harm to his person or in any other manner deceive him or harm his property, which is on this island . Because I am ordering each and everyone of you that from this moment onward that the cited island of Cabo Verde is mine and that the aforementioned Mr. Antonio da Noli is my captain on it and that the other inhabitants on the island are my vassals and natural subjects and that you will protect, treat and help them and favor them as my own vassals and do not forget that as I have previously stated that you will not bring any harm to him or his property, so you will be responsible for defending all of this and ensuring that nobody makes any claims on it, nor takes, nor steals nor kills or otherwise causes any other type of harm or deceit upon them (the islanders) or their possessions. And for all of you, this letter will be well known and that none of you can claim ignorance because I am ordering that this letter be displayed publicly in all of the squares and markets as well as any other places in the cities and towns where people customarily congregate. Anyone who commits any act in opposition to this letter will be dealt with by the criminal justice system under the most severe of penalties. This letter is written in the town of Medina del Campo on the 6th day of June, in the year of our Lord Jesus Christ, in 1477. I am the King. I Gaspar de Aryno, the secretary of the King, our highness, have written this letter by his order.

And still another important detail to understand, is that it was not only mariners that came to the capital of Cabo Verde. There were also other passengers on these ships, merchants from the Portuguese kingdom and Spaniards and their agents who went to the coast of Guine, the Indias de Castela and to Brazil in search of the riches that this new sea route might bring them.

I hope that we now know a little more about the history of Cabo Verde and the Hispanic community. Now I will explain a little about the culture of Cabo Verde itself. Cabo Verde was an important laboratory where they experimented with a mixture of many cultural influences, a melting pot for a new human type in both language and mentality: the Creole was born through the fusion of whites and black slaves and eventually other races as more and more diversity reached the islands.

The fact is, that in order to settle and occupy the islands, beginning in 1462, it was necessary to introduce everything, men, animals, foodstuffs from Portugal, Africa, Brazil and India. In the interior of the islands, slave labor was utilized, They farmed dry arable lands with corn and beans and irrigated land for sugar cane. Coffee, cotton, tobacco and horse and livestock raising, began as an experimental laboratory in the development of Cabo Verde. Afterwards, all of this experience was transferred to the new territories of Brazil, New Spain and the West Indies, etc.

So, when one sees the cultures of the Hispanic and Lusophone communities, we will usually find many similarities and many of these similarities have their roots in the Cape Verde Islands, because it is here where these communities began to develop.

All of this information shows that Cabo Verde and Cape Verdeans were instrumental in transferring Africans and culture to the new territories of America whether dominated by the Spanish or the Portuguese.

Later, many of the Africans in these countries became Hispanics. Unfortunately, today many of them know nothing about these origins and practically nothing about Cabo Verde and the role that she played in this phase of their lives. That is why I believe that it is very important to disclose this information to everyone, especially for Hispanics of African

50

descent to create a basis for them to study their past. The hope is that others will be enlightened to seek new programs in schools that will harmonize relations between the two groups (Hispanics and Lusophones).

But of course this will not be easy, because millions within these groups consider themselves to be victims of the adventures of the catholic kings with the blessings of the Pope. Therefore it is also necessary that we understand the past in order to determine the direction of our future. And it is in this direction that I hope we can work together so that this project can be realized.

There is no lack of materials for research, the only thing that is lacking are those concerned individuals to develop this subject. I believe that the Cape Verdeans should cooperate with the CPLP (The community of Portuguese speaking countries) to link this history with all members of the community. Hopefully we can create an export market for cultural and historical products, especially with the help of organizations that are interested in the conservation and exposure of the history of the expansion of western civilization during the discovery period.

Besides this we would like to create a geographical area where all members of the human race can settle and live without racial problems, while attracting investors who will have confidence in this system.

It is very important to understand that in Cabo Verde people have learned to live in harmony with each other, because they had to survive together on these islands in the middle of the ocean and after several centuries they are not concerned about someone's race. It is truly a spectacle for strangers who do not understand this way of life, because here the melting pot is different, because it is here where a new mestizo race began.

Finally, we must also remember that Cabo Verde played a major role in the transfer of European settlers to South America through the port of Porto Grande on the island of Sao Vicente and by the international airport on the island of Sal.

Although this assistance was given in the 19th and 20th century, their descendants who are now called Hispanics or Lusophones are probably completely unaware of the services provided by the Cape Verdeans in their destinies.

Practically all of the emigrants from Germany, Italy and England who went to Brazil, as well as other parts of South America and South Africa at a time when Europeans were increasingly coming to discover and settle in new geographical areas had to pass through Porto Grande, Sao Vicente, right up until the end of the 19th century. As we shall see, many more passed through this port in the 20th century.

The poet, Sergio Frusoni, was the son of Italians who came to Sao Vicente in the 19th century. He was born in Mindelo in 1901, and his poetry, which was written entirely in Creole, portrays more so than anyone, the spirit and character of the people of his native island Sao Vicente.

Cabo Verde was directly involved with both Africans and Europeans in the settlements of South America and the development of the Hispanic and Lusophone worlds.

Navigational companies with monthly stops in Mindelo. Cabo Verde

Navigational companies with monthly stops at Mindelo, Cabo Verde

Company	Nationality	Route
Empresa Lusitania	Portuguese	Lisbon - Madeira - S. Vicente - Bolama - S. Tomé - Angola
Royal Mail Steam Packet Co.	English	Southampton - Lisbon - Brazil - Rio de Plata
Pacific Steam Navigation Co.	English	Liverpool - Lisbon - Brazil - Rio de Plata - Valparaiso
Orient Steam Navigation Co.	English	London - Cape of Good Hope- Australia
Lamport & Holt	English	Liverpool - London - Brazil - Rio de Plata
Societe General de Transports Maritimes	French	Marseille - Brazil - Rio de Plata
Chargeurs Reunies	French	Le Havre - Brazil - Rio de Plata
Apestiguy Freres	French	Bordeaux - Brazil - Rio de Plata
Dufur Ebruzza	Italian	Genoa - Brazil - Rio de Plata
Societa Lavarrelo	Italian	Genoa - Brazil - Rio de Plata
Rocco Piaggio & Filho	Italian	Genoa - Brazil - Rio de Plata
Nicolo Schiafino	Italian	Genoa - Brazil - Rio de Plata
Nord Deutscher Loyd	German	Bremen - Brazil- Rio de Plata
Hamburg Sudamerikanische Gesellschaft Kosmos	German	Hamburg-Lisbon-Brazil- Rio de Plata
Dampschiffahrt Gesellschaft Kosmos	Germany	Hamburg-Rio de Plata- Valparaiso

| Societe Generale de Transporte Maritimes | France | Marseille-Brazil-Rio de Plata |
| Chargeurs Reunies | France | Le Havre-Brazil-Rio de Plata |

Source: Joaquim Viera Bothelho da
Costa, Adiamento aos Relatorios da
Administracao do Concelho de Sao
Vicente, between 30 Jan 1877 and 1 Mar
1880

During the 1860's the port authorities
registered an average of 50,000
passengers in transit per year. In 1888
there were 170.000 passengers registered.
Obviously this was a significant
contribution to the historical and cultural
transformation of these new areas.

General Movement of Goods and Passengers in Cape Verdean Ports between the years 1930 and 1933:

TOTAL MOVEMENT

Year	Number	Tons	Crew members	Passengers*
1930	7,158	9,608,814	146,274	28,556
1931	7,517	10,415,909	162,033	29,037
1932	7,949	9,293,647	140,989	46,743
1933	7,923	7,161,263	118,673	21,096

The average movement of passengers in transit during these years was 31,000 +.

This information shows the impact of international aid provided by the Cape Verdeans during the process of global westernization with the passage of Europeans through the Cape Verde Islands, because the overwhelming majority of steamships were of European origins, especially; German, Dutch, Italian, English, Portuguese and Greek during this period.

Reference: Informacao Economica sobre o Imperio, Cabo Verde - 1934

Commercial Coal for Refueling Steamships

Porto Grande was one of the most important ports in the world in 1890, and only three other ports imported more coal than this port in Sao Vicente during the month of January of this year, these were Malta, Port Said and Singapore among the 74 coaling stations that existed in the world.

The strategic importance of Sao Vicente was based on its location in the middle of the ocean between Europe and South America. Thus it was more advantageous for supplying coal and other necessities for long trips. The competitors for this market were the Canary Islands and Dakar, Senegal, but Sao Vicente had a more centralized position on the Europe and America route, while the Canary Islands was much further north and Dakar further to the east. The five most important ports in the world, importing coal during this period were 1-Port Said, 2-Malta, 3-Singapore, 4-Sao Vicente (Cabo Verde) and 5-Genoa.

Rank	Port	Tonnage
1	Port Said	89,880
2	Malta	42,832
3	Singapore	38,688
4	**S.Vicente (Cabo Verde)**	**36,638**
5	Genoa	36,315
6	Gibraltar	34,245
7	Colombo	29,636
8	Rio de Janeiro	28,688
9	Bombay	25,989
10	Aden	21,248

Reference: Estudo sobre o comercio do carvao by Joao de Sousa Machado- Lisbon Imprensa Intl 1891

Note: Porto Grande had made a major contribution for European emigrants traveling to South America and the English had established the first coal company there in 1851. Companies with English names in 1891 were : 1 - Millers & Corey's* Cape Verde Islands L. 2 - Wilson Sons & C. , L. and 3- Companhia S. Vicente de Cabo Verde or better known as , S. Vicente (Cape Verde Islands) Coaling Company Limited.

* I found this name to be interesting to me personally, because I remember Cape Verdeans with this name living in the United States and thought that this was an unusual name for Cape Verdeans, but now I understand it better.

Closing Comments

We must always remember that much of the secret information during the discoveries was already known by the Africans and then refined by the Christians after their crusades in Africa.

Many books , maps and other documents were seized from the Muslims after these wars and once they were translated into European languages, they provided invaluable information to launch the discoveries. So, Expo-98 should be an opportunity to disclose much of this information as regards this phase of the discoveries. Perhaps certain African countries such as Morocco could provide some data in this area.

Fortunately there will be many countries participating in Expo-98 and many of them have been directly affected by the discoveries. Large and small countries such as Brazil, Mozambique, Sao Tome, India, China, Japan, Cuba, Haiti, Timor and so many others. The Portuguese were in all corners of the earth during this period, including such diverse places as Mikmakik (a territory in the Atlantic Provinces of Canada) and California.

Clearly there remains a lot of history yet to be developed. Perhaps now we can take another look at this history with the hope of finding solutions to old problems. After all the wars and atrocities that have been committed in this world, we would like to see a century of peace, while building new relations with serious countries in this endeavor. For this reason it is very important to develop the tourist industry to learn more about the history of these countries, while appreciating the problems that these nations must face today. In this way we hope that some people will try to improve the conditions for others on this planet.

This book has been written to establish the importance of Cabo Verde in the history of the discoveries, but it has always been an important history that has always been ignored in the past. But now we have plenty of information to confirm the importance of this history and to establish it permanently as a subject of major importance in schools and universities around the world. In the meantime, we do not want to forget the other countries and their contributions to this history. The truth ,is that we would like to see them develop their history with their own views about the discoveries; perhaps then, by working together, we will have the opportunity to make the world a better place.

Notable Personalities

Antonio da Noli

navigator - cartographer - 1419 - 1497

He was the 'official' discoverer of five islands in Cabo Verde in 1460. He was also the founder of the first European city in the tropics - Ribeira Grande in 1462 on the island of Santiago. He was born in Noli, in the vicinity of Genoa in 1419 and died in Cabo Verde in 1497. **He became the first Cape Verdean** along with his brother Bartolomeu and his nephew Rafaelo. The island of Santiago was known in Lisbon and other cities of Europe as Antonio's Island during his tenure as governor of Cabo Verde. **He opened the way for a new sea route to India by circling the African continent, as well as opening the way for the discovery of Brazil.** Old maps indicate that he had a strong influence on Christopher Columbus.

Diogo Afonso

He was the scribe for the king and the one who was assigned to the northern portion of the island of Santiago as the king's authoritative representative and the city of Alcatraz was founded in his name in 1462. **He discovered the last seven islands of Cabo Verde** sometime between 1461 and 1462.

Vasco da Gama

He made the celebrated voyage to India by way of Cabo Verde in 1497. And **he owed the success of his famous voyage to Antonio da Noli, who opened the way for the discovery of this route in 1460.** He well understood the importance of Cabo Verde and wrote a letter of instructions for Pedro Alvares Cabral to emphasize the necessity of going to Cabo Verde, when he (Cabral) made his famous discovery of Brazil.

Henry Mendes

Henry 'The Navigator' Mendes, 1880-1969. This famous navigator was the captain of the famous schooner 'Ernestina', named after his daughter and carried thousands of Cape Verdeans from Cabo Verde to the United States. He made 55 Atlantic crossings. The schooner was donated to the United States by the government of Cabo Verde as a lasting memory of the historical ties between the United States and Cabo Verde. Now it is recognized as a national historical treasure in the State of Massachusetts and it is also certified by the US Coast Guard as a sailing school

Captain John Sousa

A famous Cape Verdean sea captain, who was named **captain at the age of 18 when he sailed his first boat to America**. For the greater part of 40 years he made an annual voyage between New England and Cabo Verde. He died in 1958 at the age of 75.

Captain Jose Lima

The brave seaman who managed to make it across the Atlantic in the small sail boat the 'Nettie', to the island of Brava (Cabo Verde), on a voyage that took 57 days between 3 July and 30 August, 1935. His boat had been caught in different storms and miraculously everyone survived the ordeal and he received a hero's welcome in Cabo Verde.

Captain Joseph Manuel Lopes

Sailed the schooner 'Capitania' in 1942 between New England, Africa and Cabo Verde.

Almicar Cabral

1924 -1973 - The political leader of Guine-Bissau and Cabo Verde. One of the most famous Cape Verdeans who was a liberator of African colonies from Portugal. His campaign to liberate the colonies was very similar to that of Simone Bolivar in South America. He was assassinated in Conarky on 20 January 1973.

Captain Pedro Evora

He commanded various Cape Verdean boats in the 40's and 50's between Cabo Verde and America. He was the last captain of the famous schooner 'Ernestina'.

Columbus

A man of many mysteries, but nevertheless, some phases of his life have been relatively clear. He was very knowledgeable of the importance of Cabo Verde in his voyages and few historians will dispute that fact. There is little doubt that he travelled to Cabo Verde and almost certainly would have known Antonio da Noli, as all the evidence indicates that he was well aware of the importance of Antonio da Noli. Columbus himself made references to Cabo Verde and Antonio da Noli on several occasions; in his own handwriting; on maps and in his ships' logs.

59ʼ

Roberto Duarte Silva

1837 - 1889. A famous scientist - He was born on the island of Santo Antao in 1837 and died in Paris in 1889. **He was the president of the Chemical Society of France.** In 1876, the Academia Real das Ciencias of Lisbon elected him as their member correspondent. This academy still maintains some of his original letters and other works written by him. There is a monument in his honor in the cemetery - Pere Lachaise (Montparnasse) France.

70

61

Eugenio Tavares: 1867 - 1930

A famous poet and writer during the period that preceded 'Claridade' (the Enlightenment- Period) in Cabo Verde. He was a native of the island of Brava and died in 1930 at the age of 63. His mornas are songs that are sung around the world in many countries, even today. One of his most famous songs is 'Hora de Bai' a sad song that is often sung at the end of a performance or when friends and relatives are departing. He was considered by many to be 'the conscience of Cabo Verde' during the period of much of its suffering in the first half of the 20th century. He also lived in Onset, Massachusetts for a few years.

In the Voz de Cabo Verde in 1912, he appealed to his readers to defend the Portuguese republic and that they be given all the rights and responsibilities of Portuguese citizenship and he appealed to the republic to eliminate the disgraceful situation of the blacks and that each native be transformed into a citizen of Portugal (in 1914 ALL cape verdeans had become portuguese citizens).

There was a Homage to Eugenio Tavares in Lisbon in 1997, sponsored by the City Hall of Lisbon and the Eugenio Tavares Foundation. Organised by the Eugenio Tavares Foundation and the President of the Camara Municipal de Lisboa it took place at the Videoteca de Lisboa at 3:00 P.M. on the 25th of January 1997. This session commemorated the memory of the 120 years since the birth of the famous Cape Verdean poet and also paid homage to the poet Rodrigo Peres on the occasion of his 80th birthday.

Volume II

The 'Missing Pages' of Hispanics and Blacks in history

THE CHURCH

It is necessary to say a few words about the church and religion. For two reasons, firstly, because we already know that much of this expansion was related directly to the church and secondly, because many Christians were forced to accept the church (as were slaves, Indians and Jews), it wasn't always a natural or voluntary act. Thus, we must understand a little about the truth with many questions to study.

For example, why did the Europeans believe that they had the right to convert everyone to their religion? They certainly adopted a superior attitude to the indigenous peoples of America, Africa and Asia. Slavery was also a natural business for the church authorities. Therefore, we see relics and artifacts throughout the church with European representations. In this way many people have come to see the statues and paintings of Europeans as representative of the religious order and in our lifetime we see that all the Popes of the Vatican have been Europeans while there are millions of Christians who are not Europeans.

But the Catholic Church will tell us that the selection of the Pope is a divine act of God and thus a natural process. So, in other words, they tell us that it is only natural that Europeans are superior to the rest of the world.

Christianity doesn't take into account the social economic effects upon societies that have resulted from the church symbols. It seems that the American Indians initially understood the reality and meaning of nature as they worshipped the sun or the moon. So they did not have to worry about the color of God. But unfortunately, many people now think that God is a European, since that is how he is portrayed in many paintings.

And unfortunately, often times when non-Europeans accomplish something important, these accomplishments are frequently attributed to Europeans, with the attitude that they are the rightful proprietors. Thus, the history of the world is poorly written and we would like to tell a little of the truth regarding this history. **The truth is, we find mestizos, Arabs, Africans, Hispanics, Asians, Indians etc., making significant contributions to world history, but they often do not get credit for their own history.**

Here I'm speaking mainly about Europeans and the western world, because I do not know much about the other countries, while clearly there are other problems in other parts of the world.

But one of the most important objectives of this report is to let the world know that there are people who wish to live a natural life whenever possible. They wish to live alongside others without worrying about race, culture or religion. If people wish to join a religion that appeals to them, it should be a natural will, made voluntarily and not forced upon them by the church or some kind of governmental policy or any other unnatural means of enforcement.

Finally, we would like to study the evolution of humanity so that we can move forward in this millennium without repeating mistakes of the past, particularly those made during the period of Discovery.

In order to learn a little more about the church in the involvement of this expansion, the 'The Jesuits and the Mission of Cabo Verde' 1996, by Nuno da Silva Goncalves, Broteria, Lisbon explores this subject and there are also many documents in the Biblioteca da Ajuda in the National Palace of Ajuda in Lisbon. This book by Goncalves can also be found at the Sociedade de Geografia de Lisboa and in other libraries in this city.

According to author of 'MACAU-1996', Almerindo Lessa, the Pope partitioned the world between the kings of Portugal and Spain, and the Treaty of Tordesilhas opened up a new political cultural environment that was defended by the Council of the Indias, which gave it a Hispanic Catholic jurisdiction that would be worldwide in scope. Hernan Cortez carried a text written by the jurists of the Palacio Rubios when he went to Mexico. In this text the Spaniards informed the Indians that God had created one man and one woman whose descendants covered the entire world and instructed one of them to govern the world as a superior prince, unto which all mankind must obey, thus he was the head of the entire human lineage and was known as the Pope and he had awarded all the islands and the continents of the ocean to the king of Spain, and for this reason Cortez demanded that the Indians accept their situation as vassals to these kings as they were already obligated to do so.

This is a lesson in marketing that today's businessmen should study. After five hundred years we are still having problems in trying to understand this deal, but it clearly had a tremendous impact on the world.

So it would be this treaty that the Pope made between Spain and Portugal, that would determine the fate of much of humanity. This treaty made a fundamental impression on the development of various political divisions, as a minimum:

* The beginning of the Euromundo Project, the europeanization of the world that would ultimately place the whole world under the governance of the western powers, all from the white race.
* A form of papal colonialism structured much like today's United Nations.
* A turning point for the concept of International Relations and the development of a rational 'jusnaturilismo'.

Reference: "Tratado de Tordesilhas de 7 de Junho de 1494" - Adriano Moreira, Legado Politico da Ocidente: O Homen e o Estado, Lisboa 1988, page 15 , Macau by A. Lessa.

Unfortunately the church was also involved in controversies between the Portuguese kingdom and the Vatican. Especially so after the death of Bishop D. Frei Pedro Brandao in 1607, who was in the center of controversies with his role in illegal commercial activities at least since 1594. Various witnesses apparently knew that the bishop had sent ships to the coast of Guine and other ports of call and obtained merchandise for sale in Cabo Verde throughout these years. After his death, there began a long legal process to determine the claims against his estate. In this case it was determined in a letter of 28 Jan 1610, that all of his estate would go to his successor in the diocese in Cabo Verde; D. Luis Pereira de Miranda:

Letter of Relaxation 28 Jan 1610*

'As we shall see from this letter of relaxation on the confiscated property, we hereby make it known that **we are satisfied that the estate is being delivered to the Reverend Bishop Dom Luis Pereira de Miranda, the Bishop of Cabo Verde**, all of the goods in his estate, money , silver and gold pieces, **slaves** and everything else, including rights and shares that remain after the death of Dom Pedro Brandao, who was the bishop of Cabo Verde".

These issues would continue to plague the church and the Kingdom of Portugal because there also were claims from the family of the deceased Bishop D. Frei Pedro Brandao who already had a portion of the estate in their possession. Ironically, here we find a battle between the government and the church to determine the rightful ownership of the slaves. A classical legal case.

This information is based on the book 'Os Jesuitas e a Missao de Cabo Verde', mentioned previously. For this story the author (Goncalves) found documents in the Vatican Secret Archives and in the Vatican Apostolic Library.

* *Reference: Carta de Relaxacao (Gaspar Albertori), 28 Jan 1610, Biblioteca de Ajuda in Lisbon (BAL) Document No. 51VIII -9 f. 1635 (G.Albertoni was the pontifical representative in the Camara Apostolica assigned to Lisbon and communicated this letter based on guidance that came from Rome.*

Carta de Relaxao 28 Jan 1610,
copy of original, courtesy of:
Biblioteca de Ajuda in Lisbon

Summary of the Papal Bull 8 Jan 1455, regarding Africans and slavery.

This Papal Bull was written by Pope Nicholas V and is a demonstration of the methods taken by the church to dominate and control the Africans during this period. In this particular case the Pope authorized the Portuguese to invade and enslave the Africans who were considered to be infidels. Many more Bulls were written that would continue to enslave the Africans in this process. This document in its entirety is located in the National Archives of the Torre do Tombe (ANTT) in Lisbon.

The Bull – 8 January 1455: Romanus Pontifex of Pope Nicholas V conceding to D. Afonso V and his successors and to the Infante D. Henrique the conquest, occupation and appropriation of all the lands, ports, islands and seas of Africa, from Capes Bojador and Nun to Guinea, inclusive, and off the whole southern coast to its extreme point. In all these lands they may impose laws, penalties and prohibitions, and may found monasteries, religious houses and churches, whose patronage will rest with them. **Further they may reduce infidels to slavery and may invade, conquer and occupy any lands of the saracens and pagans.** The Bull forbids all Christians from navigating and fishing in the aforementioned seas, and from trading in the said lands and with their inhabitants, unless previously licensed by the King of Portugal and the Infante D. Henrique. The License assumes the payment of tribute. Nicholas V further makes mention of the great efforts, pains and expenses of D. Afonso V, the deaths of his subjects, the navigations and discoveries organized by the Infante D. Henrique, the settlement of the islands, the conversions of infidels, etc.

ROBERTO DUARTE SILVA

(1837-1889)

Roberto Duarte Silva was one of the greatest chemists of his time and was born on the island of Santo Antao in Cabo Verde on the 25th of February 1837, the son of Francisco Jose Duarte and Matilda Rosa Silva, he had two brothers Joaquim and Antonio. In his youth he came to Lisbon to begin his apprenticeship in the a pharmacy. He trained in Lisbon at the pharmacy of Alves de Azevedo, in Rossio (this is near the train station Rossio at the end of Avenida da Liberdade in the center of the city). At the age of 20, he passed a pharmaceutical exam and by unaminous consent was awarded the highest possible classification.

That same year he was awarded another distinction: **The Portuguese government sent him to Macau to establish a new pharmacy in Asia for Portugal. Three years after having completed this assignment he decided to go out on his own and establish another pharmacy in Hong Kong.**

France and England had declared war on China at this time and he came across a French squadron in Hong Kong, and obtained permission to supply the squadron with their pharmaceutical requirements. He gained the respect of all the French and they advised him to go to France and study in a more intellectual environment. Since he was rather ill and suffering from fevers and bronchitis he accepted their advice and left for France.

In Paris he continued his studies and made several trips to London where he analyzed mineral samples from his native land - Cabo Verde. He always believed that there were ways to make economic use of these minerals to support the economy of Cabo Verde. This group of islands is made up of volcanic rocks and sand and suffers from constant droughts, which caused much suffering over the centuries. So he always maintained contact with Cabo Verde and constantly tried to solve the economic problems of the islands with his scientific studies.

In France he studied French, Latin, mathematics and physics. Here he earned his Bachelor's Degree in science and became licensed. In 1867 he published his first work about compound aminos.

In 1873 he became Chief of the Department of Practical Chemistry at the School of Central Arts and Manufacturing in France. The famous chemist Friedel was his professor and helped him obtain this position.

Throughout all of these triumphs he was a sickly man in frail health, with even worse disastersto come. Not least, the loss of his left eye, the result of a laboratory explosion. He knew that he would have to lose the eye or risk going totally blind.

In 1876 The Academy Real das Ciencias in Lisbon elected him to their staff of advisory correspondents.

In 1878 he was appointed a member of the Portuguese jurors at the Universal Exposition in Paris while judging the works of his country in the competition by applying an innovative audaciousness. For that effort **he was awarded the Legion of Honor Cross and the Degree of Cavaleiro de Santiago (Knight of Santiago).**

In Paris he created the Municipal School of Chemistry and Physics and was appointed as one of the professors.

In 1887 he was elected as President of the Chemical Society of Paris. This was the highest honor that he could possibly obtain, and the fact that he was a foreigner (a Cape Verdean), made it even more unusual and rare, such was the quality of his works that he was appreciated and deeply respected by the intellectual judges of the world.

During the night of the 8th and 9th of February 1889, he passed away and the world lost one of its most famous chemists, the Cape Verdean Roberto Duarte Silva, and his funeral attracted famous personalities from all over the world to pay final respects to this great man.

A special report was inscribed by Antonio Augusto de Aguiar and the physicists and chemists Thomaz de Carvalho, Barbosa du Bocage, Ferreira Lapa and Augostinho Lourenco, which paid tribute to Professor Silva. At the same time an official document was made of his biographical sketch to show his accomplishments.

His contemporaries said that he was an indefatigable worker despite his constant illness. In the cemetery of Montparnasse, there is a funeral monument at his grave site with the simple inscription that reads, 'To Roberto Duarte Silva, from his students his colleagues and his friends, the Chemical Society of France'.

In 1937, the School of Arts and Manufacturing of Paris celebrated the centenary of his birth together with the Academia Real de Sciencias de Lisboa and they invited his nephew Joaquim Duarte Silva to take part in the ceremonies. The Academia Real das Sciencias de Lisboa still maintains letters on file that were written by Roberto Duarte Silva. In these letters it is clear that he was always proud of his homeland Cabo Verde and spoke of it often. This academy also has references on some of his publications and studies.

THE CAPE VERDEAN IMPACT ON INTERNATIONAL TRADE

D. HENRIQUE, CABO VERDE, and the NEW FRONTIERS

Professor Walter Prescott who was the deacon of the University of Texas and also served as president of the Association of North American Historians said that the discovery of America and the opening of a sea route to Asia by the Cape of Good Hope were two of the most important events ever registered in the history of mankind. And clearly, Cabo Verde and Cape Verdeans were always at the center of these events.

This argument is positively confirmed by the voyage of Vasco da Gama that opened the gateway to sea trade in the orient and brought Europe the commerce she had been seeking, This voyage was far more important than that of Columbus. According to Charles Verlinden, Columbus' trip was deceiving, since he didn't return with any goods for European commerce, but just a few poor Indians. We already know that Vasco da Gama based his voyage on direct logistical support from Cabo Verde and the Cape Verdeans. Ironically much of the history of Columbus is based on his direct experience and involvement with Cabo Verde and Cape Verdeans.

In order to establish the true history of the expansion of the western world it is clear that this phase of history was a Portuguese initiative of the Infante D. Henrique. Verlinden also explains that it was the increased command of the seas that allowed western civilization to advance. **The growth of western civilization in the modern phase is attributed especially to Portugal and Cabo Verde.** The success of this phase of history by the Portuguese was based on its strategic use of the Cape Verde Islands and the Cape Verdeans while providing the impetus for the exploration of new lands and seas. Verlinden adds that the 'westernization of the world' was a titanic movement, the most important social phenomena of modern times, which is only today being seen and understood.

It is also interesting to know that Vasco da Gama, stated that the last known civilization on his route to India was that of Cabo Verde. Therefore, it was mandatory for him to anchor in Cabo Verde on his schedule to ensure that he received new supplies and make final adjustments to his ships before beginning the great journey around Africa to India.

The modern world owes its emergence to Portugal, led by D. Henrique, which broadened both the physical horizon and mentality of Europe. At this time in history, the Turks and Arabs blocked all the land routes with access to Africa and Asia and it was this blockade that provided the incentive for a response from the west, and that was made by Portugal, by encircling the Islamic world with the adventures of Vasco da Gama as a continuation of the efforts laid out by D. Henrique.

Whether by land or by sea the Portuguese were opening up vast territories that Christianity and the West had never known before; while initiating the Europeanization or Westernization of the world; with emphasis on the strategic location of Cabo Verde; followed by the period of rapid economic growth for Europe or the 'Boom' period.

In other words the Cape Verde Islands served the Portuguese kingdom and the west as the only route to India until the opening of the Suez Canal several centuries later.

We can now say that the arrival of Vasco da Gama in India in 1498 was one of the most important events in the history of humanity, because it broke the Muslim economic blockade, bringing domination of the sea to Portugal, and moved the history of Europe from the shores of the Mediterranean. And with control over this trade route by the Portuguese, all of Europe's businessmen had to purchase their goods in Lisbon.

D. Henrique's thinking was always to break the economic dependency in which Christianity found itself. In spite of the temptations by others and the success of Columbus, the Portuguese objective was always to find a trade route to India. India consisted of all the lands from Madagascar to Sofala (Mozambique) to the east and extended up to the waters that

Magellan called the Pacific. This was the area that Europe wanted open for trade and to stimulate commerce, which had become stagnant and suppressed by the Muslims.

The world-renowned historian, Arnold Toynbee, recognized the fact that it was the Iberian pioneers (mainly the Portuguese and the Cape Verdeans) that managed to circumvent the Arab power base and open up the frontiers of the world for western development. It was these pioneers who provided a service to the West and Christianity that was without parallel. They expanded the horizons and consequently the dominion of Western society from an obscure corner of the old world to new lands that they could settle and the opportunities to explore the seas. It was from this Iberian energy and initiative that was the outgrowth of western Christianity.

In truth, with the discovery of Cabo Verde, Portugal planted the seeds that would eventually become the tree that would provide shelter to the rest of the world under its branches. Toynbee tells us that the westernization of today's world, "is a realization of the Iberian pioneers of Western Christianity, especially during the years between 1475 and 1575". These are important years in Cape Verdean history when world trade was intensified and the great discoveries were made that these islands were used as a fundamental base in order to attain the successes of Columbus, da Gama, Magellan, Vespuccio, Dias, Cabral, Pinzon and so many more. All of these navigators benefited from Cabo Verde during these 100 years.

But Toynbee also tells us that Vasco da Gama opened a new era in 1497: He called it the Gama Age, which he named after the navigator. This historical period would last until the Atomic Age began in 1949.

But all of this glory has now passed for these pioneers and today we can see plenty of poverty in the Iberian countries and much more so in Cabo Verde and other Lusophone countries, although we can find many treasures of the past especially in the museums of Portugal and Spain. The history of Cabo Verde is very rich and represents a great lesson for the western world to study. Many Cape Verdeans would like to see the world take this history into account in order for others to learn firsthand the roots of the modern day world of today and how the West made its expansion around the globe.

EXAMPLES OF INTERNATIONAL AID

In this section are listed a few examples of international aid furnished by Cape Verdeans, in addition to those already mentioned, because much of this information is virtually unknown to the descendants of those who actually received the aid, especially Afro -Americans, the US Navy and Brazil and other countries.

Aid was furnished by Cape Verdeans to the United States of America and the US Navy, led by Commodore Perry during the mission to suppress the slave traffic on the west coast of Africa and also to help American blacks who wanted to return to Africa in the 19th century

(reference: Old Bruin - Commodore Perry - by S. E. Morrison, page 67).

Perry describes the island of Santiago, Cabo Verde, saying that, "the island has the capacity to provide an abundance of corn, coffee, cotton, sugar and indigo, but that the Cape Verdeans only work as hard as is absolutely necessary. But they do produce enough of a supplement to make it a favorite stopping point for ships going to the Pacific or Brazil".

Perry also made a map of the port of Praia and circulated it within the Department of the Navy.

Perry's comments and observations about Cape Verdeans are very interesting and extremely important, because he apparently recognized the intensity of the aid supplied by cape verdeans to international ships going to Brazil and those that had to go around Africa to the Far East.

At the same time it appears as though he expected much more support from the Cape Verdeans. The reality is that Cape Verdeans provided as much support for the Americans as they did for other countries and in this concept the benefits were much more advantageous to the foreigners than for the Cape Verdeans themselves, while the foreigners were enriched as a general rule the Cape Verdeans became poorer.

There were some Americans who thought that Commodore Perry and the African Squadron under his command were wasting their time in Cabo Verde in the middle of the ocean when their mission should have been on the continent of Africa if they were going to suppress the slave trade. But Morrison tells us that the African Squadron of the United States received unjust criticism for spending time in Cabo Verde because the reality was that they were ordered to do so. There weren't any other ports along the African coast that were considered healthy and secure for the American fleet. Commodore Perry explained it rather well when he said that, "between the Gambia river and the equator you could not establish a naval base, and any attempt to do so, would result in very serious consequences for human life and without any benefits for Liberia and could cause a lot of resentment back in the United States that would be a setback for the colonization efforts".

Perry goes on to tell us that in order to clothe and feed a thousand sailors for two months, required substantial warehousing to maintain supplies. He stressed the fact that, "without any doubt, Cabo Verde was the base that was the most secure in order to perform this mission" which was to help the Americans and their project to settle black Americans in Liberia. Besides this, the African coast was considered very dangerous for white people who were not accustomed to living in a tropical climate.

Perry purchased a tract of land in Porto Grande to establish a cemetery for those Americans and Englishmen who died during this mission.

Scientific Investigation: Commodore Perry brought back some curiosities which were presented to the scientific academic community. The National Institute received a bread fruit and a curious species of fish from Cabo Verde for the promotion of science.

These examples of assistance are based on the previously mentioned book 'Old Bruin' by S. E. Morrison and took place in the 1840's. Morrison clearly establishes Cabo Verde's logistical role in the colonization of Liberia, by those black Americans who wanted to return to Africa.

Brazil was also another country that received substantial aid from Cape Verdeans and Cabo Verde as we have already learned, yet it is noteworthy to highlight the comments of Colonel Gaspar do Couto Ribeira Villas, a Portuguese army officer who wrote in his book, 'The Portuguese and Colonization that, **"it was Cabo Verde who supplied a major portion of the livestock that was shipped to Brazil during the colonization period of that country"**.

Finally, it is also extremely important to note that the Portuguese Ministry of Education has published a booklet 'Olhares sobre Cabo Verde', in which is stressed the involvement of Cabo Verde in the European settlements of South America, South Africa and Australia. This information is significant, because now there seems to be an atmosphere of cooperation between Cabo Verde and Portugal in disclosing the true history between the two countries. Obviously, it is virtually impossible to teach a history lesson in a Portuguese school that glorifies Portuguese history without mentioning Cabo Verde and the contributions of Cape Verdeans and the other Lusophone countries. Hopefully this cooperation will serve as a model for other colonial countries around the world who have suffered from similar problems. I suspect that this may well be the case with the Indians of North and South America who may have lost most of their history in the colonization process. Naturally this situation also applies to Afro-Americans whether in North America or South America in addition to other areas such as the Caribbean, etc.

THE JEWS AND CABO VERDE

The Jews represented about 20% of Portugal's total population in 1497. There were about a million Portuguese inhabitants at that time and about 80,000 of them were established Jewish residents, when in 1492, Spain evicted Jews during the Inquisition and 120,000 went to Portugal.

In 1497 practically all of these Jews were converted to Christianity by the will of the Portuguese government as Judaism 'officially' ceased to exist in the country. All the Jewish tombstones were said to have been destroyed at that time. The tombstones of the Jewish cemetery Almocavar were given to the hospital 'Todos os Santos', which was destroyed later by an earthquake.

The first Jews to settle in Portugal in modern times are believed to have come from Gibraltar and Moroccos at the beginning of the 19th century. These were the Sephardis. The first Ashkentis came around 1910.

With a high concentration of Jews it was only logical that some of them went to Cabo Verde. Perhaps, even some of the great navigators may have been Jews, especially Pedro Alvares Cabral, who Jewish historians consider to have been one of the 'New Christians' (those Jews converted to Christianity). In any case, Jews did make up part of the history of Cabo Verde as did many other nationalities and today there are Jewish tombstones in several cemeteries to confirm this history.

Jewish Cemeteries in Cabo Verde

1. Praia, Santiago - has a small separate cemetery for Jews.

2. Ponta do Sol, Santo Antao - has many Jewish tombstones in the community cemetery.

3.Campinas - Penha de Franca, Santo Antao - has six Jewish tombstones.
4. Paul, Santo Antao - has an area managed by a non-governmental organization .

This information was taken from 'World Guide for the Jewish Traveler' by Warren Freedman, E. P. Dutton Inc., NY 1984.

SOME PROBLEMS WITH HISTORY

No. 1

The 'National Geographic' magazine has written many outstanding feature stories about Columbus, and slavery and the Discovery Period. However, in a curious story in a publication of 1992 a map was published by William Graves showing the various slave routes taken by the slave traders and nothing was mentioned about Cabo Verde. An extremely important omission, because this reflects a tendency in the teaching of history; the omission of perhaps the most important segment of the teaching of the Discovery Period and the after effects that are still taking place around the world today. It also makes it very difficult for people of Afro-American descent to trace their past. Fortunately, in another article published in another edition of the same magazine, a map was published showing many of the famous Portuguese discovery voyages has many discovery voyages passing through Cabo Verde. This is an important inclusion because it establishes a direct link with Cabo Verde and the discoveries around the world. It was after all, imperative that these ships stop in Cabo Verde for logistical (water, provisions, repairs, etc.) and moral support, whether going to, or returning from, their destinations, because these islands were prepared to provide these services. In fact, without these services many ships would not have reached their destinations.

SOME PROBLEMS WITH HISTORY

No. 2

A newspaper article printed in 'The Standard Times' in New Bedford, MA on 3 December 1993 stated that the Senior Editor of the American 'TIME' magazine, Barret Seamen, had printed a special edition of this magazine to show the world how the United States was starting to become the world's first multicultural society and representing the people of the future.

Mr. Seaman said that Cabo Verde was not considered because, "the population is so small" and added that, "Cabo Verde was not in the same league as the United States in sheer numbers".

In fact, Almerindo Lessa in 'MACAU', Lisbon, 1996, page 25, tells us that Cabo Verde is a demonstration of the first known Euro-Afro-Asian civilization.

While Leopold S. Senghor, writes in 'Biologia and Mesticagem' Evora 1989, "that world wide racial mixing started with the great discoveries in the 15th century and the African slave trade (through Cabo Verde)... The mestizo is the only new feature of modern anthropology and that the luso-tropical mixed breed (American, African and Asian) is an unmistakable sign and an eternal mark of our passage through history. We have even created a national policy for mixed race peoples. The seeds (of race mixing), were planted in the 15th and 16th centuries according to Joao de Barros, in such a way that still today it astonishes modern genetics."

PROBLEMS WITH RACE MIXING AS SEEN BY AMERICANS

The world generally does not understand the mentality of race relations in the Lusophone community and some other countries. In the year (1997), in the United States, a country with a history of segregation and racial discrimination, Americans still have many racial problems. The famous golfer, Tiger Woods, still a young man has had to face many problems simply because he is a mestizo (Indian-Black-Asian and

Caucasian). Powerful Americans want to classify him as Black without any thought whatsoever about the psycho-sociological impact on his family or on the American community. Mr. Woods has clearly stated that he is proud of his racial heritage as it is; Indian , Asian , Black and Caucasian. Even President Clinton became involved in the act by inviting the golfer to participate in ceremonies honoring American Black heritage, truly a noble cause indeed.

However, it is fairly safe to say that the President would never have entertained the idea for Mr. Woods to participate in say an Asian heritage celebration. In the meantime many Asians are also proud of Tiger Woods, as are many Blacks. Many of us will have to learn to share our ethnic experience and be proud of it as it is without causing undo harm to others.

Certainly , Mr. Wood's comments made on TV will bring more attention to the historical problem in the United States where racial classifications are outdated, especially as the American census of 2000, did not consider mixed race people as a category. Many people are not given the opportunity to select their appropriate race. For example, in Texas, one is often forced to choose between Black and White without any other possibilities. This may sound incredible, but it is true. Many people find this system to be very offensive.

I believe that Lusophones have had a history of intense racial mixing for more than five centuries and therefore should have the right to enjoy the naturalness of their race in a friendly environment. We expect to find this environment in the Lusophone community, but perhaps we also still have a lot to learn. The worst situation for someone born in the Lusophone community is when one must live in another country and be subjected to racial policies that are offensive and not to have any recourse to resolve them. This is especially true for the Lusophone community because of its history of intense race mixing throughout the centuries. In this situation many people will be forced to lose their culture, their language and their pride which is the inheritance given by their parents. This history is obviously an extension of the glory of Portugal, whether it be Afro-Portuguese, Indian-Portuguese, Asian-Portuguese or simply Lusophone,. The Lusophone culture is always linked in this history despite problems of the past. So the responsibility for protecting this history and culture should be with Lusophone agencies whether governmental or non-governmental.

If we want to reflect on the Lusophone culture we must protect the Lusophones in all categories. This should be the reason to improve upon relations within the Lusophone community throughout the world. It is very difficult and practically impossible to give justice to the glory of Portugal without including everyone within the Lusophone community.

Naturally there is a lot of information missing from the history of Cabo Verde and other Lusophone countries. That is why I have written this book.

UNPUBLISHED VIEWS OF CABO VERDE

by Colonel Ribeira Villa

Os Portugueses na Colonization 1929 - Lisbon, Professor of the Colonial Superior School.

In this section it is necessary that the world get an opportunity to gain some insight of the Portuguese scholastic system in describing Cabo Verde and Cape Verdeans. The writings of Colonel Villas provides us with a rare insight of what appears to be either official or quasi-official views of Cape Verdeans and some of their history that was written in the 1920's. By understanding these writings, we can learn a lot from the past, as I have personally found this information to be extremely interesting as well as important to the student of Cape Verdean history.

CABO VERDE

The archipelago was discovered in 1460. The islands were deserted like the others that have been discussed (Madeira and the Azores), and as with these islands, they were also given as an endowment to the royal family of the Algarve, including slaves from Guine. By the year 1500 these settlers would be joined by condemned exiles and in 1601 with new Christians (former Jews).

Santiago and Fogo were the first islands to be colonized. Freed slaves and or runaways settled the other islands (These runaway slaves often settled in the interior of the islands away from the colonizers and would eventually become known as 'badius', taken from the Portuguese word 'vadio' which means vagrant or vagabond. This word has often been used in America by the Cape Verdean community in naming some Cape Verdeans, such as 'Tony Badiu' or 'Jack Badiu', now with this knowledge, the American Cape Verdean community will have a better understanding of their history.).

The islands would incorporate all of the European and tropical cultures. The population would raise livestock and anything else that would be of interest to passing ships that would stop over for water and provisions.

It was Cabo Verde that supplied a major portion of the livestock that was sent to Brazil during the colonization period.

It became the diocese's headquarters for the Bishop beginning in 1532, the very same year that Pizarro began his conquest of Mexico. The colony had been linked to Guine for a long time because of the commercial importance for the archipelago, so it was reserved for trade along the coast of Africa (Guine). That's the way it had been since 1462.

For this reason the people of Cabo Verde sent Andre de Almeida* to Lisbon in 1580 to deal with the settlements of Serra Leone (this was a part of Guine during this period), and in 1690, the Company of Cacheu appears in Cabo Verde encircling the two colonies.

In Cabo Verde, a native black and mestizo population took hold and assimilated into a totally European culture; mainly in their way of living. The Metropole worker (those from Portugal) was superior to the Cape Verdean worker.

Christianity was somewhat isolated but with a European quality that would maintain these beliefs. (Here I think that it should be pointed out to the reader, that Portugal is said to have prohibited slaves from mating with those of the same tribes from Africa, so their historical traditions would ultimately fade away as they took on a new culture. Traditional African elements such as the beating of drums was strictly prohibited because this was a means of communication between the Africans that the Portuguese apparently feared. It seems as though the American colonizers would apply many similar methods in stamping out the culture and traditions of the American Indians, although their methods were probably much more violent and inhumane, nevertheless they probably became influenced by the methods that were applied in Cabo Verde).

Cape Verdeans are hard working, intelligent and have produced; government officials, soldiers, and scientists. They have been employed as farmers and as seamen, and being outstanding whalers. Many emigrate, but they return to their homeland, they are knowledgeable in French and English while striving to improve their lives with their meager earnings. Statistics show that in one year the island of Brava, with 10,000 residents received $100,000 coming from the USA in registered mail.

In many parts of the world, one can find examples of this type of colonization. Once the primitive slaves came in contact with and were managed by the Portuguese, their way of life was completely transformed, including their mentality, becoming like Europeans. As **is a fact that deserves to be studied and which should be brought to the attention of sociologists,** especially those who are quick to judgment without having studied the facts about Portugal and the truth based on poor assumptions.

The Cape Verdean black is a descendant of Guine, and without cross breeding, has differentiated himself completely from his race, being today a well civilized element of society in life's struggles, with an intense national spirit, always saying, that he is a Portuguese from Cabo Verde. They even recognize this in the United States (early 20th century) where there are many Cape Verdean settlements.

Note: Colonel Villas says that the black Cape Verdean did not cross breed while differentiating himself completely from his race, but as has already been noted, it appears that they were forbidden to mate with members of the same tribe and it must be remembered that Guine consisted of a much larger area in the 15th and 16th centuries than is known today. So it is very possible that they may have bred with other Guineans, but they could have been from a tribe from Serra Leone or Gabon, etc.

This characteristic represents a new feature of colonialism, showing, still another important phase of progress, being one more clear testimony of her (Portugal's) colonial abilities.

Cabo Verde was by accident a difficult location to colonize. But her backwardness and the hindrances that she suffered, when undergoing full development, was in fact a political problem. It was international piracy, that was glorifying privateering, razing, and sacking the islands whenever they (pirates) encountered them on their routes. Adventures of this nature would hamper growth and development in Cabo Verde.

97

Note: In this case many students of history will probably remember reading about pirates like Francis Drake, who was honored in England and glorified in American history books. Drake would be accompanied by hundreds of bandits, while plundering Cabo Verde in addition to his other exploits of infamy.

Given the situation of Cabo Verde; an international seaport, a population that preferred to live in the port areas along the coast, but who were attacked and robbed by pirates, or sometimes they would emigrate or perhaps withdraw to the hills, in this way, almost all of the settlements along the coast were abandoned in order to escape the threat of pirates.

And in the 16th century the so-called pirates began their visits which continued for a whole century while bringing to a halt the development of Cabo Verde, that otherwise would have taken place much earlier as was the case with Madeira and the Azores. However, if the archipelago could say something about 'Portugal in the History of Colonization' more would be said about the honorable foreigners who lived off the labor of others, not having provided civilization and humanity the eminent service expected and prevented the advancement of the colonization of Cabo Verde and in this way did justice due the pirates. One can see who really was the colonizer here.

Cabo Verde now has about 6,000 Whites, 90,000 Mestizos and 55,000 Blacks.

Institutions in Cabo Verde: there is one high school, 110 primary schools and several professional schools (for pilots, navigation, fish, agriculture and industry).

These figures are for the late 1920's.

The capital city, Praia has nice solid buildings almost like those in Europe, it doesn't resemble anything like those improvised colonial cities and therefore my traveling companion was amazed to see it. He also happens to be from Sarvognan de Brazza and is enroute to the Congo.

Sao Vicente (Porto Grande de Mindelo) has one of the most important ports in the world and with its situation is destined to be of major importance, both commercially and strategically. It represents an excellent naval base for the South Atlantic. It caught the attention of the famous colonial, Colonel Joao de Almeida of the Corpo de Estado Maior, who carefully examined the operations of this port in such a way that it will satisfy, the most demanding requirements, whether they be commercial or military.

*Apparently this name is incorrect and should have been Andre de Almada the Cape Verdean captain and knight, according to A. Teixeira da Mota in his book 'Two Fifteenth Century Cape Verdean Writers - Andre Alvares de Almada and Andre Dornelas'. Junta de Investigacao do Ultramar, Lisboa, 1971. This is an important revelation because it shows that Andre de Almada was a very important Cape Verdean who had the respect of the Cape Verdean community in 1580. Since Francis Drake attacked the islands in 1585 it appears that it is very possible that Andre de Almada may have defended the islands against Drake and his pirates. In the next story written by Colonel Villas we shall see that this same individual (Almada) was also a mestizo and was awarded the title of the Knight of Christ in 1603 because he was an outstanding soldier who defended the islands against the continuous attacks by the enemy.

CABO VERDE

This is another unpublished article by the same author, Colonel Villas.

This archipelago located west of Cabo Verde off the west coast of Africa (the readers should be aware that there is another Cabo Verde, a promontory on the African coast), from which it gets its name, was reached by Antonio da Noli , who discovered (1457) five islands, during the life of the Infante (D. Henrique), while the rest of them were discovered by the Infante D. Fernando's scribe, (1461-1462), Diogo Afonso, just after this Infante conferred upon him the 'Mestrado da Ordem de Cristo' (the Military Order of Christ - this was a foundation that was founded in 1417 in Portugal to fund expeditionary missions of this sort and is immortalized by the famous red crosses displayed on the sails of Portuguese caravels during the Age of Discovery), an organization founded by his uncle, Inclito Henrique.

The base for the departure point of the discoveries would naturally be the coast (of Africa), so one can see why the first island to be reached was the island of Boa Vista, the most eastward of the group (of Cape Verde islands), and therefore the closest to the coast of Africa.

The archipelago would have a great future due to its location in the ocean, which was certainly a compulsory port of call for ships heading not only to Brazil but also to Asia: the importance of which would only be significantly reduced after the opening of the Suez Canal when it took over as the preferred route to Asia. Its value was based on this factor (location), even though it was a good distance from Portugal and did not offer the agricultural possibilities as did Madeira. This evaluation began with the island of Santiago by a system initiated on Madeira which partitioned the island in two parts between two grantees known as Capitais - Donatarios and these were the discoverers: Antonio da Noli, who received the southern part and would establish Ribeira Grande as its capital and Diogo Afonso who received the northern part with the town of Alcatrazes as its capital. These types of Land Grants (Capitanias-Donatarias) were unknown before that of Goncalo Velho in the Azores at the time when they were created. They were aware of this documentation. But the concession of the land grants would have to succeed in order for the discoveries to take place. In this way, the navigators would not ease up on their exploratory missions, which was to learn as much as possible about the South Atlantic. These captaincies (land grants) allowed the discoverer to rule the land as the Governor and served as an incentive to explore the seas. Consequently, the documentation by the King D. Afonso V concluded that the land grants would be effective beginning with the date of settlements, which was considered to be in 1462 (for Cabo Verde). And since manual labor (here the author is obviously referring to slave labor) from Guine was already there in 1461, it must be this date that the Donatarios actually started taking on the arrival of the first settlers: an important date indicating the era in which the base was created to discover the South American Continent (Brazil). And naturally the first grants already being 'the Grand Master of Christ' (Grao Mestre do Cristo) the Infante D. Fernando and the contemporaries of his grants (the island of Terceira-Azores), to Alvaro Martims and Jacome Bruges.

Note: I find that the name Bruges is interesting here because it appears to be a reflection of the involvement of the Flemish in Portuguese history. There is a very important city named Bruge in the Flemish area of Belgium and I strongly suspect there is a direct relationship between Jacome Bruge and that city. It is also interesting because many Flemish navigators and settlers were very much involved in the early stages of the history of Madeira and the Azores and they are believed to be part of the first European settlers in Cabo Verde.

Antonio da Noli settled permanently in his captaincy as a settler and resident, accompanied by his friends, his brother Bartolomeu and his nephew Rafaelo along with other genoese, probably crew members aboard the ships that came with him from Genoa. It seems that Diogo Afonso did not follow the same path of development for his share of the island but instead delegated his part to others. The settlement was made with couples from the kingdom (of Portugal) , mostly from the Algarve in the beginning, and later there would be those who were condemned to exile and the New Christians. The method of manual labor that was adopted by all of the colonial peoples, would be the black slaves, that would come from the coast of Guine. It seems as though this would have been the case in 1461, and also the captured moors (from Morocco), the consequences of the Moroccan War. With the passing of time and the increased wealth of the islands, there would be upper class foreigners settling here, besides those already working in commerce, but these however did not reside on the islands. One such example were the merchants from Seville, Joao and Pero de Lugo, coming from the Canary Islands, and were authorized in 1464 to explore the urzela plant (a plant used for dye and grown in Cabo Verde) and transport it to Seville and Portugal.

This mestizo population is extremely interesting, integrating in the life of the continental, with commercial trade conducted by the native islanders (Cape Verdeans), they are intelligent, hard working, living entirely as Europeans, having great relations with the population that was formed in Brazil, which is verified by the many points of contact between Cape Verdean and Brazilian poets, as can be seen in their compositions.

The first important document - Foral - actually the Carta Organica da Ilha, emanating from the King D. Afonso V in 1465, showing that at the time when the Flemish came to the Azores, the development attained by Santiago was good enough to justify elevating it to a higher administrative level. **The settlement consisted of Whites, Arabs, Blacks and Mestizos**, a judicial system, commercial trade being conducted throughout Guine except for Arguim, being a true monopoly for the people and ships of Santiago, only people of status being able to purchase blacks there (Guine); this trade was extended to the Canary Islands, the Azores, Madeira and the Kingdom of Portugal, the economic importance of the island was defined by the officials of the Crown in their treatment of taxes on the island; i.e., tax exemptions for the colonizers of Santiago, the method that was applied to intensify local development. This document shows that the population development in Cabo Verde was greater than that of Guine, thanks to the maritime importance of the archipelago; thus, there now was a predominance of economic groupings formed between Guine and the island.

In complying with Portuguese tradition, the church was there to provide spiritual needs for the people, setting up chapels and parishes as this was directed by the Infante, it seems to invoke the Holy Spirit. This was pretty much the cult of the Middle Ages and that had almost disappeared in the Kingdom. The first monks came in 1466 (shortly after the Foral document was written), with the arrival of Fr. Rodrigo and Fr. Jaime, from the Order of San Francisco, belonging to the Convent of San Bernadino of Atouguia, both of them being of Catalan origin (from Spain), it seems that they had been assigned to Madeira previously. This was to be the nucleus of the future Casa da Ordem (House of Order) a missionary to unite the first settlers, especially for the conversion of arabs and blacks. They (the monks) knew that they lived in poverty and one of them, Frei Rogerio who was about 70 years old, was ordered assassinated by Bartolomeu da Noli (Antonio's brother), for making his female companion abandon him, because they were living together in the Kingdom. Bartolomeu was supposed to have been delivered to justice, but we don't have any more info on this case (nevertheless as we have seen earlier in the chapter about Antonio da Noli, Frei Jaime was blamed for the crime and imprisoned but was eventually released because the settlers were angry and an uprising was feared).

But what is curious about all of this is that it happened in 1466 while Bartolomeu was registered as the Captain of the island as Antonio was absent. He could have been in the Corte (court), but given the fact the Noli family had complete control of the captaincy (Capitania), one might suppose that Antonio was away at sea and navigating the Southern Atlantic, a task more compatible with his temperament as a seaman.

As the island progressed, the King named a tax collector to initiate fiscal accountability to be made to the Crown (1471), and the Perfect Prince (Principe Perfeito) (1480) gave him new privileges. It appears that this is the reason for the existence on the island of; wind mills, saw mills, equipment for mining, salt exploration, soap factories, the distribution of uncultivated land to the islanders (which shows that the islanders were living in conditions in which they were now willing to commit themselves to the cultivation of the land), apparently the raising of livestock (the animals were allowed to roam freely on deserted islands, etc. So it can be seen that the task of increasing the value of the island would not be stopped. After the death of the Duke of Viseu, the islands would revert to the Crown (1484), but later in 1489, they are granted to the Duke of Beja, Mestre de Cristo, the future successor of the King D. Joao the II.

Diogo Afonso died and his captaincy was passed on to his nephew, Rodrigo Afonso as a grant in 1485, by the previously cited Duke of Beja, which he himself confirmed in 1496 after he was crowned King, a document that becomes the new Carta Organica for the island.

As a consequence of the grant, Rodrigo promoted wild livestock raising on the island of Boa Vista in 1490 and the first settlers were black shepherds coming from Santiago and perhaps some others coming from the coast (Guine). The island was granted to him for that purpose, and it seems that he was also granted the island of Maio for the same reason, but Rodrigo Afonso sold it, and it was passed on to others. Somewhat later, couples from Santiago came to the island of Fogo; and opportunely, there appeared descendants of Rafaelo da Noli who established themselves on the islands of Fogo and Brava (Brava has a town at the top of the mountain named after Joao da Noli).

Antonio da Noli died in 1496 (Italian history books state that he died in 1497) without any male heirs and only had a daughter named D. Branca de Aguiar. Because of the 'legal mentality', due to lack of a male heir, the captaincy would under normal circumstances revert back to the King since females could not inherit property of the Crown. However, an exception was registered for this captaincy and it would be conferred to D. Branca, contingent upon her marrying a gentleman to be chosen by the King*, who would govern the island of the deceased Noli. It was Jorge Correia de Sousa, a nobleman from the House of the King (Casa do Rei) who was chosen for his previous services rendered. He would say that in 1497, a year after the death of Mister Antonio, that his daughter's grant was a reward to conserve the captaincy of her father, but that it had to have a nobleman in the lineage.

Nothing is reported in the history of the services rendered by the selected husband, but perhaps he could have been an assistant of the deceased (A. da Noli).

But **the services of da Noli in the colonization of Santiago were real, since he was the creator of the archipelago and civilized it. His most notable services was to turn Santiago into a sea base, while broadening the scope of his navigational endeavors and investigating the South Atlantic to a greater degree than anyone in the history of navigation,** thereby simplifying it for those who were absorbed in the 'Ciencia de Sagres' (the famous school of navigation in Portugal that was renowned for the development of the great navigators in history) and would be involved in the discovery of the coast that would become the future Brazil. This is a hypothesis that should be considered as a possibility.

*This exception to existing law is an emphatic demonstration of just how important Antonio da Noli was to Portugal, thus making it inevitable that historians will eventually begin to do more research on this famous cape verdean in the near future. Obviously his stature retained a profound impact on the Crown of Portugal even after his death.

Since Jorge Correia de Sousa was the son of Joao Correia de Sousa of the Order of Santiago, he also held the insignia of Aljezur. From the marriage of the noble gentleman and the daughter of Antonio da Noli, came an illustrious generation, beginning with their son,, Belchoir Correia de Sousa who succeeded him as Governor (Capitao-Donatario), Joao Correia de Sousa, Commendator of the Order of Christ who was the Captain of Calecut (India), etc. With these titles, one starts to see more of the Cape Verdean influence in India and Asia.

Of interest for the protection of Cabo Verde on behalf of the King D. Manuel we get to see his determination (1497) to erect a hospital, with the goal that its maintenance be reverted to its heirs, who it seemed would be many, from the deceased colonists without, a last will. During the time of that King, there was a monopoly on soap manufacturing and also on wild livestock raising. Rodrigo Afonso (previously mentioned) was developing the cotton industry for export.

One can say that these 36 years (1461-1497) produced colonial labor, so that it would be put on the path to enhance the value of the archipelago of Cabo Verde, that was once a group of deserted islands and uncultivated, that under the guidance of the colonists, the labor force, especially blacks, transformed it and giving it a valued agriculture. This was connected to the trade in Guine and the development coming from the hospitality of those ships crossing the South Atlantic, being another source of income.

This hospitality has been expressed by the voyage of Vasco da Gama: in 1497, the Admiral anchored at Santiago where he remained for six days, taking in water supplies (actually he took on new provisions and made vital repairs to his ships during this stay, for which the crew was very grateful). From here he separated with Barolomeu Dias*, who sailed in waters in which he was more familiar and Vasco da Gama would then sail to the South Atlantic, a voyage that would finally conquer science.**

* Apparently, the reader can see the intensity of some of the activities of Bartolomeu Dias who accompanied da Gama to Cabo Verde and then departed his company to go on with his own explorations. Dias it should be remembered, had already rounded the Horn of Africa in 1488, by sailing along the coast of Africa and reaching the Cape of Good Hope, so he was very familiar with these waters and perhaps that is the reason that he accompanied da Gama to Cabo Verde. Vasco da Gama, of course would be taking a different route than Dias, as he would be sailing in the open seas and not along the African coast. Dias would actually return to Cabo Verde in 1500 with Pedro Alvares Cabral to make the second voyage to India and taking the route made famous by da Gama, but unfortunately Dias and his crew were lost at sea after departing Cabo Verde on that fateful voyage in 1500. So while that particular voyage would make Cabral famous for the discovery of Brazil, it was also the last voyage for the famous navigator Dias who was lost at sea.

** It must also be noted that in making this voyage to India at this time, that not only was it the beginning of modern capitalism because of the international trade that was developed, but it also had a definitive impact on science and navigation as the world learned about the scientific nature of the seas, as well as new lands, geography, air currents, astronomy etc.

And the development of Cabo Verde would continue, by 1513 Santiago continued its slave trade, as ships preferred to stop and purchase slaves on the islands rather than on the Coast of Guine; exports to Spain and Portugal consisted of: ivory, wax, rice, leather, and goat skins, while importing in exchange; flour, biscuits, wine, hats, pants, woven cotton cloths, caps, olives, china ware, figs, raisons, canvases (used for making sails), etc. Santiago even exported cattle, beans, salt, fat etc. The number of slaves exported from 1513 - 15, mainly through Ribeira Grande is estimated to be about 3,000. Cotton was exported to Flanders (Belgium and Holland) by 1515 (once again I believe that it is noteworthy to point out the involvement of the Flemish in the history of Cabo Verde, because normally this phase of Cape Verdean history is unknown). And besides the Portuguese, there were foreigners doing business in Cabo Verde (Santiago); the colonists of upper status exceeded 25 people in the captaincy of Alcatrazes and in Ribeira Grande this number was 75; from whence came two branches of the descendants of the Governor Antonio da Noli, including the wealthy Joao da Noli, Knight of the Order of Santiago (1515).

By 1515 the population of the captaincy of Alcatrazes (the main town), started to decline and the residents preferred the port of Santa Catarina da Praia. This captaincy, perhaps because it was somewhat abandoned by its leaders, could not advance as did Ribeira Grande, while from there, the settlers would also move to Praia because this port was proving to be more useful for sea traffic. So that by 1536, the authorities themselves were transferred there (Praia) and this facilitated its growth, due to the abandonment of the old central locations in the captaincies that were created by Antonio da Noli. The ruins of this city (Ribeira Grande) are now called Cidade Velha. These ruins represent the Golden Ages that were attained there by the end of the 16th century, while showing unmistakable signs of Portuguese dominance, a well defined effort by Portugal that created it. One can still see the remains of the cathedral, the bishop's standard (his symbol of authority), the hospital and the Holy House of the Misericordia of the Franciscan monks (Capuchos), 3 churches, walled court yards, a fortress and other fortifications.

This remarkable colonial prosperity, so new and so quick, was accomplished in 57 years (1461 -1518), it received a serious setback in 1518 as it had many of its privileges from the trade with Guine, reduced, that was a real monopoly due to the excesses practiced by the Cape Verdean tradesmen on the Coast of Guine, excesses which called for the intervention by authorities to police the traffic, showing that the Crown was not forgetting to properly organize the administration of such an important colony.

The colonial organization surged under D. Joao III and with his efficient staff, would effectively create the true beginnings of Brazil by 1530, the date that is usually accepted (although Brazil was discovered in 1500, it wasn't until two or three decades later that the Portuguese intensified colonization there). Cabo Verde had already shown its value for the execution of this phase of the Portuguese colonial operations and Martim Afonso de Sousa was entrusted with the responsibility to implement the royal instructions as the first Governor of Brazil. He stops in Cabo Verde where he installs the Capitao-Mor (the principal island authority or Governor), the magistrate, judges and he distributed annexed lands to the colonizers. This operation must have taken place throughout that entire year, since the fleet of Afonso Martim de Sousa departed the river Tejo (Lisbon) in the first days of December 1530. D. Joao III still established in Cabo Verde, proof of its development, the following authorities: land managers, administrators for orphans, notaries, attorneys for the deceased and absentees, accountants, customs agents, Commander of the Sea etc. The cotton industry on the island of Fogo was regulated by 1532, the year in which the Pope, Clemente VII established the Diocese, this is proof of the christianization of the islands and the African coastal areas, since this Bishop in Cabo Verde had jurisdiction over Cache, Bissau, Zeguichor, Farim, Geba, Rio Nuno, Gambia, Serra Leone etc. (these were all areas that were part of the Coast of Guine during this period).

By 1587 during this growth, the top island position of authority had been elevated to Capitan-General, Commander of the Armed Forces and Governor, with separation between civil authority and the judiciary. The prosperity of the colony can be seen by its receipts:

INCOME STATEMENT

Total Revenues	16,881$614
Less Expenses	5,138$014
Net Profit	11,661$386

This represents **an enormous net profit of 69%** and is a clear indication of the value of Cabo Verde to the Portuguese Crown.

The situation in Cabo Verde regarding its maritime traffic of the South Atlantic trade routes would wipe out the prosperity that was attained, reportedly, due to regular military attacks, and others by pirates or from those pirates who were ravaging the seas and concentrating in this area.

And by this time there was a mestizo named Andre Alvares de Almeida, the son of a white Portuguese man and a black woman. He wrote the first history of the region in his book, 'The Brief Treaty of the Kingdom of Guine and Cabo Verde' (1594). But he exemplified himself as a guerrilla, defending the islands from continuous enemy attacks, in such *a manner that despite being a mestizo and although it was against the Estatuto da Ordem (Statutory Order), the successor of the Templars, in 1603* **he is honored as a Cavaleiro de Cristo (Knight of Christ):** *very likely, the highest honor ever awarded in the history of colonialism, to a native, with the spirit of a continental Portuguese.*

OTHER ISLANDS

It was in 1469 that the famous Fernao Gomes da Mina made a contract with the Crown to take on the life of a Portuguese colonial on the Coast of Africa in exchange for his services to the state. He would be allowed to take care of his commercial business while at the same time he would be making discoveries in each one of the five years that the contract lasted, 100 leagues from the location (of Serra Leone)., which had been reached by the scribe Pero de Pinto. In this adventure he would reach Gabon, Soeiro da Costa, arriving at the river that it was named after, joining the Axem, which became a commercial center for gold. The gentlemen; Joao de Santarem and Pero de Escobar would go to Mina where they erected a Castelo which had a view of Benin. As a consequence of this effort J. de Santarem and P. de Escobar discovered the islands of Sao Tome and Ano Bom (1470). Lopo Goncalves found the island that would be called Principe and the nobleman Fernando Po (1486?), the island Formosa that was given the name of the discoverer: Island of Fernando Po. Sometime later the Armada da India (1503) discovered the island of Santa Helena.

These islands were not as good as Cabo Verde, but more or less fundamentally like those of Madeira and the Azores: therefore they represented a bona fide discovery as a consequence of the care taken in the study of navigation in the South Atlantic that would become known as the Route to India, and they could be used , at least theoretically, in the event of any unforeseen problems.

Cabo Verde and Sao Tome and Principe were very important, owing to their location. This was not the case with the rest of the islands, which did not have the same attributes or have any value that could be used immediately.

Ano Bom an uninhabited island like the other islands already mentioned, was only used by S. Tome for fishing, until in 1503 when it was given to Jorge de Meio, who didn't settle it and sold it to Luiz de Ramos de Esquivel. It has ruins there that can be seen on the east coast of the island where people were living when the Dutch attacked Fernando Po.

110

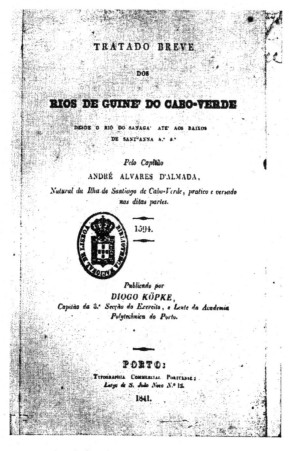

TRATADO BREVE

DOS

RIOS DE GUINE' DO CABO-VERDE

DESDE O RIO DO SANAGA' ATE' AOS BAIXOS
DE SANT'ASNA &.ª &.ª

Pelo Capitão
ANDRÉ ALVARES D'ALMADA,

*Natural da Ilha de Santiago de Cabo-Verde, pratico e versado
nas ditas partes.*

1594.

Publicado por
DIOGO KÖPKE,
*Capitão da 3.ª Secção do Exercito, e Lente da Academia
Polytechnica do Porto.*

PORTO:
TYPOGRAPHIA COMMERCIAL PORTUENSE:
Largo de S. João Novo N.º 12.
1841.

Portada do Tratado Breve *da edição de Diogo Köpke*

Cover of book written by Captain Andre Alvares
de Almada, published by Diogo Kopke

111

Andre Alvares de Almada

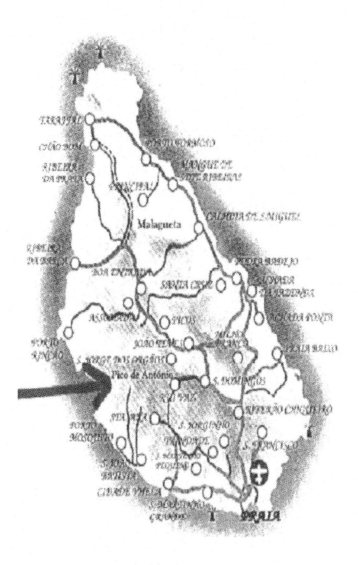

On this map, one can locate the **"Pico de Antonio"** in the southern half of the island. This peak was named after Antonio da Noli and is the only geographical name with a direct reference to him in Cabo Verde.

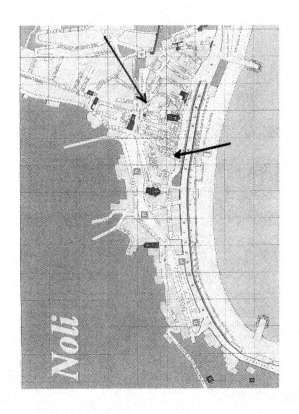

Map of Noli - Italy - Ancient Maritime Republic

Noli is a historical town, because it was one of the original maritime republics in Italy along with the likes of Genoa and Venice. Here we find; **via Anton da Noli and via Colombo** in the central part of the town. It is also interesting that, the via " Anton da Noli" runs close to the via "Colombo" but not quite touching it. That seems to be almost symbolic of the two navigators; by following the paths of both, you always seem to wind up very close to one or the other.

TRATADO DE TORDESILHAS

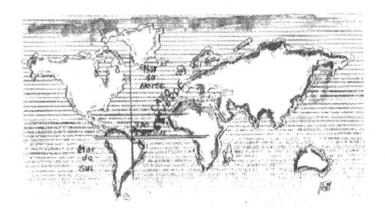

Treaty of Tordesilhas - Map of World
Division between Spain and Portugal

CABO VERDE

The Central Theme of the Treaty of Tordesilhas

Cabo Verde was extremely important for Portugal in the Treaty of Tordesilhas with countless benefits. This archipelago had an enormous impact on this treaty for many reasons:

1. It is situated in a strategic location in the Atlantic Ocean and was well known by map makers and seamen.

2. It was under the jurisdiction of the Portuguese and settled by Africans, Europeans, Arabs, mestizos and Jews as Cape Verdeans.

3. With this control, the Portuguese could control key points on the African coast.

4. With the 'official' discovery of Brazil, they could extend this control to South America.

5. With the control of Brazil and Africa, they had a route without any significant rivals for the trade in India and Asia (that which was desired by all the Europeans in order to stimulate their stagnant economies which had been suppressed by the Muslim blockade).

6. During all of this time the Cape Verdeans on these islands had to serve the Portuguese kingdom by the king's order to supply and repair all the ships of the kingdom heading for Brazil, the African coast and to the Orient and those returning from these points. Thus it would be a base for mariners of the kingdom with an enormous impact on world trade. Because of this, it has been considered as one of the greatest events in the history of mankind (according to such historians as Arnold Toynbee and Charles Verlinden among others).

116

7. Portugal also had the opportunity to discover countries that were otherwise unknown in Africa and Asia, after the discovery of Brazil.

8. For the two Iberian countries and the Vatican it was a great opportunity to expand outside of Europe with their religion (the catholic church), that would come to dominate the culture of 500 million people that live in these countries today.

9. The Portuguese and Spanish languages would become established as official languages in these countries as well as the laws of Portugal and Spain.

10. This treaty became the basis for the creation of the Hispanic and Lusophone societies that exist today.

11. Many names of states and cities in the countries of Asia, America and Africa outside the Lusophone and Hispanic countries also have Iberian names, for example; California, Florida, Colorado, Nevada, Sierra Leone, Cabo da Boa Esperanza, Labrador, Formosa and Australia.

When reading the Treaty of Tordesilhas and finding that Cabo Verde is mentioned as a dividing line between Portugal and Spain for the dominion of these oceans and lands, we are unable to comprehend the full meaning of this text. It is obvious that with these key points just mentioned, we can see that Cabo Verde was far more important than just a dividing line in history between Portugal and Spain, because without Cape Verdeans on these islands to serve the kingdom of Portugal the treaty would have been worthless. The Portuguese displayed true genius in their ability to benefit from the employment of Italians and Cape Verdeans in their dominance of world trade and colonialism that would last for centuries. So the Treaty of Tordesilhas served them well. Also remember that the Vatican and Spain received enormous benefits from this treaty, yet it is probable that none of the beneficiaries have openly recognized the contributions of Cabo Verde and the Cape Verdeans that made it all possible. Admittedly Portugal, Spain, Brazil and Cabo Verde did commemorate the 500th anniversary of the treaty with a special stamp collection, while Portugal and Cabo Verde also minted a special coin collection in 1994. Examples of these collections are in this book as testimony to the importance of this event.

Now we must try and find a way through the educational systems around the world to explain these events so that people will have a better understanding of their past that will provide them with a path to their future.

We should also remember that not only was the Treaty of Tordesilhas centered on Cabo Verde and Cape Verdeans but that this is also where modern day capitalism began as we have seen as a result of the voyage by Vasco da Gama. All businessmen and women as well as historians, geographers, anthropologists, sociologists, navigators, aviators, cartographers, military personnel, foreign service personnel, religious leaders, political leaders and other types of educators will want to know at least the basic tenets of this history.

THE TREATY OF TORDESILHAS

In the name of the Almighty God, the Father , the Son and the Holy Ghost, three truly distinct and separate people of one divine spirit. Be it clear and well known for all those who shall see this public instrument that in the town of Tordesilhas, on the seventh day of the month of July in the year of the birth of Our Lord Jesus Christ in 1494, in our presence the secretaries, scribes and public notaries before writing. being present the Honorable D. Henrique Henriquez, the chief steward of the most high and most powerful princes the honorables D. Fernando and D. Isabel, by the grace of God king and Queen of Castille, of Leon, of Aragon, of Sicilia, of Granada, etc., and D. Gutierre de Cardenas, the chief accountant of the cited king and queen, and doctor Rodrigo Maldonado, all members of the council of the cited king and queen of Castille, of Leon, of Aragon, of Sicilia, of Granada, etc., and their respected attorneys on one side. The honorable Rui de Sousa, the gentleman from Sagres and Beringel, and D. Joao de Sousa, his son, the chief inspector for his highness and most eminent gentleman, the revered D. Joao, by the grace of God king of Portugal and the Algarve for whom and from overseas in Africa and lord of Guine, and Aires de Almada magistrate of civil deeds in his court and from his pledge, all members of the council of the cited gentleman the king of Portugal and his ambassadors, and respected attorneys in accordance with both sides having shown him by letters of authority and powers of attorney the respected gentlemen their constituents. From which their text is as follows, item by item.

D. Fernando and D. Isabel, by the grace of God king and queen of Castille, of Leon, of Sicilia, of Granada, [etc.]. Considering that the most serene king of Portugal, our very dear and beloved brother, has sent to us by his ambassadors and attorneys, Rui de Sousa who are from the town of Sagres and Berlingel, and D. Joao de Sousa his chief inspector, and Aires de Almada his magistrate of civil deeds in his court and of his pledge, all members of his council to execute and take note and agree with us, or with our ambassadors and attorneys in our name over the differences between us and the most serene king of Portugal who is our brother, about that which

119

belongs to us and to him, that which up until now has been to discover the ocean-sea. However, having confidence in you, D. Henrique Henriquez, our chief steward and D. Gutierre de Cardenas the chief commendator of Leon, our chief comptroller, and doctor Rodrigo Maldonado, all members of our council, those of you who in fact protect our service, carrying out orders that we mandate; by this letter, we are giving you extended authority of the highest order, which is especially required for this case, so that for us and in our name and that of our heirs and successors and for all of our kingdoms and jurisdictions, their subjects and natives, you can discuss, negotiate, and note and contract and approve with these ambassadors and the most serene king of Portugal, our brother, in his name, any agreement, notation, restriction, boundary and approval regarding that which has been indicated by the winds and degrees of the north and of the sun and by those parts, divisions and places in the sky and the sea and land that with which you are well familiar; and therefore we give you this authority so that you can leave to the king of Portugal and his kingdoms and successors, all the seas , islands and lands that shall be retained within any limiting boundary and to which these shall remain affixed. And likewise we are giving you this authority so that in our name and that of our heirs and successors and of all of our kingdoms and jurisdictions, their subjects and natives, you can approve and note and receive and accept for the king of Portugal and his ambassadors and attorneys in his name, all of the seas, islands and lands that shall stay and remain with us and with our successors so that they should be ours as our possessions and conquest, and thus for our kingdoms and their successors, with those restrictions and exceptions of which we should be well aware. And especially that which has been mentioned and for each and every single thing and part of it, and on it,, to wherever it borders and upon that which it is dependent, or to which it is attached and connected in any way, you can make and confer, approve, negotiate and receive and accept in our names and of our heirs and successors, and of all of our kingdoms and jurisdictions, their subjects and natives, and any capitulation's, contracts and covenants with any connections, acts, methods, conditions and commitments and stipulations, regrets and submissions and renunciations that

120

you would like to see. And upon which you can make and confer anything and each and every single item of any essential quality, seriousness and importance, that is or could be possessed, still that being such that by its condition it warrants another signature by us and a special mandate and that which must have been legally executed and uniquely and explicitly stated, so that we may personally, execute, grant and receive. Likewise we are giving you extended authority to pledge and affirm in our spirit that we and our heirs and successors, subjects and natives and acquired vassals, or those that may be acquired, we shall have, protect, and honor, and that they shall indeed have, protect and honor to the utmost, for which all of you should have annotated, capitulated, pledged and conferred and affirmed, taking all precautions against fraud, deception, fabrication and false claims. and so you may in our names capitulate, secure and promise, that we shall personally secure, pledge, promise and confer and sign everything that all of you have completed in our name and concerning that which has been mentioned, is to be secured and promised and capitulated within that time frame of which you are well aware; and that we shall indeed protect and honor to the utmost and under those conditions, regrets, and commitments contained in the contract of peace between us and the most serene king, our brother, executed and approved, and under all of the others, for which all of you promise and note. That which from now on we promise to pay should we become liable, for everything and every portion thereof from the authority that we are giving you, as a free and general administration. And we are promising and securing by our faith and regal word, to have, protect and honor, we and our heirs and successors, everything for all of you, concerning that of which we have spoken, that in any way would be accomplished, capitulated and pledged and promised. And we promise to be determined and impartial, agreeable, stable and protecting, now and forever and always. And that we shall neither turn against it nor any part of it, and neither we nor our heirs and successors, not by us nor by any others, either directly or indirectly under any pretext for any reason outside of it, the explicit obligations of which we are making for all of our fiscal and inherited wealth all the property of our vassals and subjects and natives that they have or may

121

have. By this firmness we mandate this letter of authority, to which we are affixing our signatures and stamping with our seal. Given in the town of Tordesilhas on the fifth day of the month of June, in the year of our Lord Jesus Christ in 1494. I, the king. I, the queen. I Fernando Alvarez de Toledo, secretary of the king and queen our royal highness, I have prepared by their order. D. Joao by the grace of God, king of Portugal and of the Algarves from here and there, overseas in Africa, and lord of Guine. With regard to this letter of authority and power of attorney we shall see, that we make it known that considering that by mandate of the most high and most revered and powerful princes, the king D. Fernando and queen D. Isabel, the king and queen of Castille, of Leon, of Aragon, of Sicilia, of Granada etc., our most beloved and precious brothers, some islands were newly found and discovered, and from now on we will be able to go forward and find and discover other islands and lands, concerning these and others that are found or may be found, by right and reason that we have in this, we and our kingdoms and jurisdictions, their subjects and natives will be able to survive the debates and differences between us to which our Lord does not consent. For our pleasure, for the great love and friendship that exists between us, we seek to find and conserve a more stable and lasting peace that is cordial and tranquil; that the sea in which these islands are located or were found shall be separated and bordered between us in a dignified, certain and limiting way. And because at this time we cannot personally understand what this in fact actually means, I have confidence that you; Rui de Sousa, the gentleman of Sagres and Beringel, and D. Joao de Sousa, our chief inspector, and Aires de Almada, magistrate of civil deeds in our court and of our guard, all members of our council, that by this letter we are giving you extended powers and authority and a special mandate that we are making and establishing for the two of you, jointly as one. Should any of the others be restricted in any way, our ambassadors and attorneys will by the best means possible at the highest levels, take action in such case (s) that requires that generalities and specifics be treated in such a way that the generalities do not alter the specifics, and neither the specifics, the generalities, so that for us and in our name and of all of our heirs and successors and of all our kingdoms and jurisdictions, their subjects and natives, you may discuss, negotiate, annotate and execute, you may discuss, negotiate, annotate and execute with the council of the king and queen of Castille, our brothers, or with whomever has the authority to represent them, in any agreement, notations and limitations, boundaries and approvals, over the ocean-sea, islands and mainland's in which they are located, as indicated by the wind directions and by the degrees of the north and by the sun and by those parts and divisions and places in the sky and the sea that you know well. And so we give you this authority so that you leave and provide to the king and queen , and to their kingdoms and successors, all of the seas, islands and lands that will be within any limitations and boundaries that are retained by these kings and queens. And therefore we authorize you in our name and of our heirs and successors and of all of our kingdoms and jurisdictions, their subjects and natives to negotiate with these kings and queens, or with their attorneys and to approve, note, and receive and accept that all of the seas, islands and lands that shall be within these limitations and coastal boundaries, seas, islands and lands, shall remain with us and our successors, these should be ours as our property and conquest, and therefore of our kingdoms and their successors with those restrictions and exceptions of our islands and with all of the other clauses and declarations that you know well. The authority that we give to you, Rui de Sousa and D. Joao de Sousa and Aires de Almada, is as has been specifically stated, and for each and every part of it, and on that which it borders and upon which it depends, and to which it is annexed or connected in any way, you may execute confer, negotiate, discuss, offend and receive and accept in our name and our heirs and successors and of all their kingdoms and jurisdictions, their subjects and natives, any capitulation's, contracts, and deeds, with any connections, pacts, methods, conditions and obligations and stipulations, regrets and submissions and revocations that you may deem necessary; you may execute and confer everything as well as each and every item individually, by any means that may be natural and qualitative, and serious and important, that is or could be, although this may be such that by its condition, it may require yet another specific mandate and so it should be officially recognized and lawfully made unique and explicitly stated, so that we can personally execute, grant and receive. And likewise we are giving you extensive authority so that you may testify and pledge in our spirit, that we and our heirs and successors and subjects and natives and acquired vassals and those who may be acquired, that we shall possess, protect and honor, and that they shall indeed, possess, protect and honor to the utmost, everything that you have noted, capitulated and witnessed and conferred and signed, while taking all precautions against, fraud, deception and false claims. And thus, you may in our name, capitulate, secure and promise, that we personally shall secure, pledge and promise and sign everything that you have taken in our name, concerning that which has been said, which is; to secure, promise and capitulate within that time frame that you know very well. And that we shall indeed, effectively, protect and honor it under the conditions, regrets and obligations contained in the peace contract between us that we executed and approved, and under all of the others that you might promise and register in our name. That for which, from now on we promise to pay, and we shall indeed effectively pay for that which we are held liable, so that for each and every thing and part of it, we are empowering you with a free and general administration, and we are promising and securing by the true faith that we have, to protect and honor and consequently, our heirs and successors, everything that concerns you that has been mentioned and that in any way would have been done, capitulated and declared and promised, and we promise to be determined and impartial, grateful, equitable, and worthy for now and forever. And that we shall not oppose it and neither shall they oppose it or any part of it whatsoever at any time for any reason, by us nor by them, nor by anyone else, either directly or indirectly, under any pretext or by any opinion outside of it, regarding the explicit commitments that we are making for our kingdoms and jurisdictions and for all the others of our fiscal and paternal estate, and any others of our vassals, and subjects and natives, all the property that they now possess or could possess. And with this testimony and faith that we are mandating to you with this letter signed by us and certified with our seal. Given in our city of Lisbon on the eight of March. Executed by Rui de Pina. The year since the birth of our Lord Jesus Christ in 1494. The King.

(1) And therefore, the previously mentioned attorneys of the king and queen of Castille, of Leon, of Aragon, of Sicilia, of Granada, etc., and the king of Portugal and the Algarves, etc., have said that, considering that between these kings and their constituents, there are certain differences, about what belongs to whom between the two sides, that until today, the day of consummating this capitulation, that is to discover the ocean-sea; however, as well as for peace and harmony, and owing to the affection that the king of Portugal has for the king and queen of Castille, and of Aragon, etc., and for the pleasure of their royal highness, and their attorneys and in their name and by virtue of their authority, having granted and consented that they execute and assign through the ocean-sea a line or a straight line going directly from pole to pole, knowing that it is from the arctic pole to the antarctic pole, which runs from north to south. For which this line or boundary, which is to be made straight as indicated previously, from **370 leagues (1,200 miles approx.) from the Cape Verde Islands, on the west side**, by degrees or other method that may be better and quicker, that can be given in a way that will not be greater. And that everything that up to here is found and discovered, from this point forward by the honorable king of Portugal and by his ships, whether islands or mainland from this boundary and demarcation line that was made in the manner stated above, going eastward through the eastern sector from the north to the south within this stated boundary in such a way that it does not cross over the stated boundary, so this shall be that which remains and belongs to the king of Portugal and to his successors forever and always. And that all of the rest, whether islands or mainland that are found and may be found, discovered and to be discovered, which are or were found by the honorable king and queen of Castille and of Aragon, etc.,., and by their ships, from the stated boundary which was made as stated above, going westward after passing this stated boundary through the western sector from the north to the south within this boundary, that everything shall stay and belong to the honorable king and queen of Castille and of Leon, etc., and of their successors forever and always.

(2) Item. These attorneys have promised and assured that from this day forward they will not send any ships, with the knowledge of the honorable king and queen of Castille, of Leon, and of Aragon, etc., from that part of the line to the east; because, there on that side; this sector remains for the honorable king of Portugal, and the Algarves, etc. Neither shall the honorable king of Portugal go to the other side of this line which remains with the king and queen of Castille and of Aragon, etc., to discover and search for lands, nor any islands whatsoever, nor to contract nor to rescue, nor to conquer in any manner whatsoever. However, that which occurs while going by necessity on this side of the line, by the ships of the honorable king and queen of Castille, of Leon and of Aragon, etc., should any lands or islands be found while traveling in this manner, these shall belong to the king of Portugal and for his heirs forever and always, and their highness shall then have them mandated and delivered to him. And if the ships of the honorable king of Portugal should find any islands or lands in the sector belonging to the honorable king and queen of Castille, of Leon, and of Aragon, etc., that all of these finding shall belong to the honorable king and queen of Castille, and of Leon and of Aragon, etc., and for their heirs forever and always. And that the honorable king of Portugal shall then have them mandated and delivered to them.

(3) Item. So that the stated line or boundary of this partition shall be as given and shall be made as straight as possible and going 370 leagues from the Cape Verde Islands to the western sector as has been stated, that being approved and noted by the attorneys on both sides, within the first ten months from the date of making this capitulation, these gentlemen and their constituents will have to dispatch two or four caravels, with the knowledge of one or two from each side; generally agreeing in principle to that which may be necessary by both sides; to a location which during the expressed time, being adjacent to the island Gran Canary (Canary Islands). And each side should dispatch in them, men, such as pilots, as well as astrologers and seamen, and any others that would be convenient. However, this should be the same, as much as from one side as from the other, and that some of the pilots, astrologers and seamen, and learned men, who are dispatched by the honorable king and queen of Castille, of Leon, and of

Aragon, etc., are to go in the ships or ships that are dispatched by the honorable king of Portugal and of the Algarves, etc., and likewise some of these men that are dispatched by the honorable king of Portugal shall go in the ship or ships that are dispatched by the honorable king and queen of Castille, and of Aragon, so much from one side as the other, so that they may jointly see and study the sea and the directions of the wind and degrees from the sun and from the north and mark off the distance in leagues as previously mentioned, while making a joint and cooperative effort by everyone that shall go in these ships, that are to be dispatched together by both sides to carry out their authority to assign the limiting boundary lines. All of these ships shall continue to sail together on their route to the Cape Verde Islands, and from there, will take up their route directly westward until they reach 370 leagues, measured in a manner in which these men shall agree, without prejudice from either side. And when they reach this point they shall make a mark; that is convenient; by degrees from the sun or from the north or by the number of sailing days, measured in leagues, or by the best method that is mutually agreed upon between the two . sides, to that line marked from the arctic pole to the Antarctic pole, which is from the north to the south as has been stated. And this data shall be marked or annotated and signed with their names, by those men previously mentioned, who were dispatched by both sides, to carry out their authority and establish the line of demarcation while each of them representing their specific side. And that this demarcation line shall have been accomplished with everyone in agreement and is to made in perpetuity and lasting forever, in order that neither side nor their successors may contradict it, nor take it out, nor remove it at any time, nor for any possible reason whatsoever. And if by chance, the stated demarcation line which runs from pole to pole, should happen to pass through some island or mainland, and at the beginning of such island or mainland there is found to be touching this line, a symbol or fortress and that straight through such a symbol or fortress, it shall continue straight from there through any other markings through such island or mainland in a straight path from that line, it shall be divided in two with each side retaining its

127

own share. And that the subjects of both sides shall not challenge the rights of the other by passing through the demarcation line on such an island or mainland.

(4) Item. Still considering that the ships of the honorable king and queen of Castille, of Leon, of Aragon, etc., must sail from their kingdoms and jurisdictions in order to reach their sector on to other side of this demarcation line in such a way that it is by necessity required that they shall have to pass through the seas from this side of the line that belongs to the honorable king of Portugal. However, it is agreed and noted that these ships of the honorable king and queen of Castille and of Leon and of Aragon, etc., may go and return, freely, secure and peacefully within this sector of the demarcation line at any time, without any hindrances whatsoever and whenever their majesty and their successors desire to do so, while crossing these seas that belong to the honorable king of Portugal. They shall be able to take a direct route from their kingdoms to any part that is within their sector of the demarcation line and to wherever they should wish to dispatch and discover and conquer and or to contract, and to take their direct routes from where they shall agree to go for any reason, to their sector, and from whence they shall not separate themselves, unless hindered by inclement weather that may cause them to separate, as well as not taking , nor occupying, before crossing the stated boundary, anything that could be found by the honorable king of Portugal, in his sector. And if anything should be found by their ships before crossing this boundary, it shall be as stated, that this shall be for the honorable king of Portugal, and their majesty will then have to mandate that this be delivered to him.

(5) And considering that it may be that the ships and men of the honorable king and queen of Castille and of Aragon, etc., may have found for their part, up until 20 days of this current month of June in which we are making this capitulation, some islands and mainland's within the stated demarcation line, that is to be made from pole to pole and in a straight line at the end of the 370 leagues west from the Cape Verde Islands as has been stated, and agreed and noted so as to avoid any doubt, that all of these islands and lands that may be found and discovered in any way up until the 20 days of this month of June, yet, still being possible that they could

be found by ships and men of the honorable king and queen of Castille, and of Aragon, etc., and considering that they could be within the first 250 leagues of the stated 370 leagues from the Cape Verde Islands, going west to the stated line of demarcation, while being within any part of it and the two poles previously mentioned, anything that may be found within this 250 leagues, while making it a boundary or straight line from pole to pole where the 250 leagues terminates, these findings shall belong to the honorable king of Portugal and the Algarves, etc., and for his successors and kingdoms forever and always. And all of these islands and lands that up until the stated 20 days of the current month of June, should be found and discovered by ships of the honorable king and queen of Castille and of Aragon, etc., and their men, or in any manner within these 120 leagues that remain which comprise the stated 370 leagues to the stated poles that may be found up until the stated day, shall be retained by the honorable king and queen of Castille and of Aragon, etc., and for their successors and their kingdoms forever and always; as it is and has to be that which would be found beyond the demarcation line from the 370 leagues that they shall be retained for their majesty as has been stated, still being that the stated 120 leagues which are within the stated 370 leagues, that these shall be retained for the honorable king of Portugal and of the Algarves, etc., as has been stated. And if upon reaching the 20 days of the current month of June, there are not to be found by these ships of their majesty, anything within the 120 leagues, and from this period onward, anything that they may find shall be for the honorable king of Portugal has been written and contained in the above.

(6) For all that has been stated and for each and every part of it, the previously mentioned D. Henrique Henriquez, the chief steward and D. Guttiere de Cardenas, the chief comptroller, and doctor Rodrigo Maldonado, attorneys of their royal highness and most powerful princes and honorable king and queen of Castille and of Leon, and of Aragon, and of Sicilia, of Granada, etc. by virtue of their authority above that they shall incorporate; the previously mentioned Rui de Sousa and D. Joao de Sousa, his son, and Aires de Almada, attorneys and ambassadors of his royal highness and most revered prince, the honorable king of Portugal and of the Algarves,

here on this side and overseas in Africa, and lord of Guine, and by virtue of his stated power above shall incorporate, promise, assure in the name of his constituents, and their successors and kingdoms and jurisdictions forever and always, that they shall possess, protect, and honor, faithfully and indeed taking full precautions against fraud and deception, fabrication, and false claims and all that is contained herein, each and every part of it. And wanting and conceding all that is contained in this capitulation, and each and every part of it, shall be protected and honored and executed, as well as that which must be to protect, honor and execute, all that is contained in the capitulation for the peace that was made and observed between the honorable king and queen of Castille and of Aragon., and the honorable D. Afonso, king of Portugal and the honorable king that is now of Portugal, his son, being prince, in the year that passed in 1479. And under these same regrets, bonds, determination and commitments in accordance with the spirit that was contained in that capitulation of peace. And it obligates that for these parties, that neither of them nor their successors, shall move or turn against anything that has been specified above, nor against anything nor any part of it, either directly or indirectly, nor in any other way whether intentional or non-intentional, that is or would be under the penalties contained in this capitulation by that peace, and the penalty paid or not paid or graciously pardoned. This commitment, capitulation and annotation shall be and remain permanent, stable and valid forever and always. In order that, everything shall consequently be protected , honored and paid, these attorneys shall in the name of their constituents obligate all the possessions of each side, including properties, inheritances, and fiscal properties that belong to their subjects and vassals, that they possess or could possess. And they should renounce any laws and rights that they could approve that would allow them to move or turn against it, each and every one of them, as stated above. And for greater security and stability for that which has been mentioned, they shall swear by God and to the Blessed Mary while blessing themselves with the sign of the cross and taking the words of the Holy Gospel which are more broadly written, in the name of their constituents, that they and each and every one of them, shall possess, protect and honor, everything mentioned above and each and every part of it, indeed, and with full compliance, taking all necessary precautions against fraud and deception and false claims and fabrication, and shall not contradict it at any time or in any way. The referenced oath shall be sworn so as neither to request absolution nor relaxation of it from our most Holy Father the Pope, nor from any other ecclesiastical envoy or prelate with the power to do so, and still, neither shall they apply their own free will in giving it. Rather by this capitulation, they are to implore in the name of the most Holy Father, the Pope, who by his holiness confirms and approves this capitulation according to the contents therein, and by expeditiously forwarding this as part of the bulls or in any of them that are requested, and incorporating in them, the text of this capitulation and putting any judgment on that which will be opposed or passed, at any time that is or could be. And consequently the attorneys shall , in their names, obligate this penalty and pledge, so that within the first 100 days, beginning from the day of executing this capitulation, they shall give to one another, approval and adjustments of this capitulation written on parchment and signed with the names of these gentlemen and their constituents, and authenticated with their leaden seals. And in the document that they will give to the honorable king and queen of Castille and of Aragon, etc., they shall have to sign, consent and concede to the most eminent and illustrious prince, D. Joao, his son. Everything that has been awarded in these two documents, are to be the same in each one for both sides to sign their names before their secretaries and notaries, thoroughly written down and with any worthy opinions that may have been advised by either side, that were made and granted in the town of Tordesilhas, with the day, month and year indicated at the top of them. D. Henrique Henriquez, chief steward, Rui de Sousa, D. Joao de Sousa, doctor Rodrigo Maldonado; licensed, Aires (de Almada). The witnesses that were present, who came here to sign their names, the attorneys and ambassadors, who conferred on this and executed the oath; the commendator, Pero de Leon and the commendator, Fernando de Torres, from the vicinity of Valhadolid, and the commendator Fernando De Gamarra, commendator de Zagre and Zinete, attendants from the house of the honorable king and queen, our royal family, and Joao Soares de Siqueira, and Rui Leme, and Duarte

Pacheco, attendants from the house of the honorable king of Portugal, summoned for him. And I, Fernando Alvarez de Toledo, secretary of the king and queen, our royal highness and of their council, and their chamber, scribe and public notary in their court and in all their kingdoms and jurisdictions. I was present for everything that had been discussed, and together with the previously mentioned witness and with Estavao Vaz, secretary of the honorable king of Portugal, who by the authority that our honorable king and queen gave him, to have faith in this document in his kingdom and who was personally present to that which was said and was requested and granted from all of the attorneys and ambassadors, who appeared before me and signed their names here, on this public instrument that I have written. That which is written on these six pages of sealed orders, have been written in its entirety by both sides and upon which will be affixed the names of those mentioned above, along with my signature and finally each category is being notarized by me and Estavao Vaz. And therefore I have registered my signature as testimony to the accuracy. Fernando Alvarez and I, Estavao Vaz, who by the authority of the honorable king and queen of Castille and of Leon, etc., authorized me to make public in all of their kingdoms and jurisdictions, jointly with Fernando Alvarez, the requests and requirements of the ambassadors and attorneys. I was present for everything, and with this trust and the documentation here, I have notarized everything with my public signature as such.

ROYAL LETTERS THAT SHOW PROOF OF THE DISCOVERY OF CABO VERDE

The first five islands, then the last seven islands

In this section it is important to understand that there are four letters between 1460 and 1497 that were written and maintained in the National Archives in Lisbon (ANTT), that when read in sequence, **they clearly demonstrate that Antonio da Noli was the official discoverer of the Cape Verde Islands (the first five islands) and that Diogo Afonso discovered the remaining islands.** Apparently there were debates over this issue in the past and several historians have been confused on this matter over the centuries, but for the first time in history all four letters are being included in the same book with a short analysis to clarify the issues that were confusing in the past.

It is also extremely important for the reader to understand, that Antonio da Noli was the first Cape Verdean in the history of the islands which were discovered by him in 1460 and that he resided there from the time that he founded the first city, Ribeira Grande in 1462. Just like the Bible tells us that Adam and Eve were the first man and woman on earth, while some people believe that other people must have started settlements on different locations, there may be those who wish to say that maybe some other people were in Cabo Verde when da Noli arrived. However, the islands were reported to have been deserted and named Cabo Verde and da Noli was in fact a citizen and permanent resident as well as the governor of the islands for over 35 years. And clearly he was from Noli in what is now Italy and now with the information that is presented herein, he will receive his appropriate place in world history as one of the most important navigators of the 15th century.

3 Dec. 1460 - This letter represents the royal grant to the Infante D. Fernando, of the islands of Madeira, Porto Santo, Deserta, S. Luis, S. Jorge, S.Tomas, Santa Iria, Jesus Cristo, Graciosa, S. Miguel, Santa Maria, **S. JACOBE, S. FELIPE, MAIAS, S. CRISTAVAO, AND LANA**.

The last five islands listed here are the first known islands of Cabo Verde and were part of a royal gift that was granted to the Infante D. Fernando after the death of his brother, the Infante D. Henrique in 1460.

This is the first known document were the Cape Verde Islands are mentioned with their original names and only these five were known at this time. The remaining islands of the archipelago were discovered shortly afterwards.

Ref: ANTT,Misticos, L.3,fl 58v-59 (Published in: Alguns documentos do ANTT,pp27-28)

19 Sep. 1462 - Grant to the Infante D. Fernando of ALL of the Cape Verde Islands.

This document was made after it was clear that all of the islands in the archipelago had now been discovered. Note that nearly two years had elapsed since the discovery of the first five islands were mentioned. **Now for the first time, there is the name of the discoverer; Antonio da Noli** as having discovered the first five islands during the life of the Infante D. Henrique, who died in 1460.

The other 7 islands are now mentioned for the first time as having been discovered, but the discoverer is not named in this document, but the names of the islands are given; Brava, Sao Nicolau, Sao Vicente, Rasa and Branca (these two are islets), Santa Luzia, and Santo Antao.

Ref: ANTT, Chanc. D. Afonso V. L. 1, fl.61, Misticos, L.2, fl.152-152v. (Published in: Alguns documentos do ANTT, pp. 31-32

8 APR 1497 - Shortly after the death of Antonio da Noli a royal letter was written to transfer his estate (the Capitania) to his daughter D. Branca de Aguiar.

In this letter, it is confirmed that da Noli was the first to discover Cabo Verde. It is apparent that there must have been some confusion or doubts regarding this matter, but the letter clearly says that, **"based on the information available, Antonio da Noli was the FIRST to discover Cabo Verde".**

Ref: ANTT, Chanc. D. Manuel, L. 10, fl.62, D. 1, Livro das Ilhas, fl.669v. (Published in: Silva Marques, vol. II, pp.477-478)

134

29 Oct. 1462 - This is the royal letter that confirms that it was in fact Diogo Afonso, the king's scribe, who discovered the other seven islands that were mentioned in the royal letter of 19 Sep. 1462. There never was any controversy on this one. Note that this letter was written only about six weeks after that of 19 Sep. 1462. This is a good indication that the islands were discovered after 3 Dec. 1460 and before 19 Sep. 1462.

Ref: ANTT, Misticos, vol. 2.º, fl.155

Note: If anyone desires a copy of the entire contents of the above letters, I will gladly send them a copy as I have copies signed by the National Archives. My only request is that the requester pay a small fee for shipping and handling expenses. I can be reached at : marcelogomes@hotmail.com – Please note that the originals are written in Portuguese and more than 500 years ago, so unless you are well versed in the old Portuguese language it may not have much value to you.

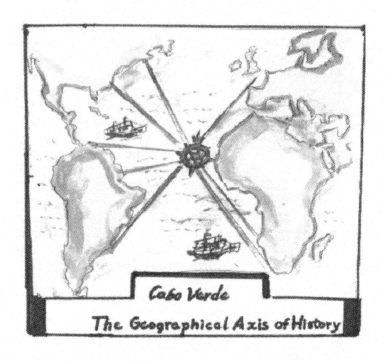

Cabo Verde

The Geographical Axis of History

The Geographical Axis of History

Cabo Verde

This is an important commentary made by Professor Mendes Correa of the Agencia Geral do Ultramar in Portugal in 1954.

In the vanguard of the great convex off the west African coast between the Tropic of Cancer and the Equator, lies the archipelago of Cabo Verde - **in spite of being located in the northern hemisphere and of its proximity to Africa - it has been in fact, symbolically and functionally, a centralized position in the Atlantic in relation to the borders of the other continents.**

Understandably the word 'strategic' best describes it - not only in the military sense but also for scientific investigations - the archipelago is strategically privileged. In respect to international communications it intersects the crossings of vital sea routes. And from the volcanic rocks that emphasize their

136

essential and decisive tectonic contours on the globe and allows for explanations that have been obscured in the dawn of history, for its people and culture, that were developed after the Portuguese occupation. There are many facts about Cabo Verde, that in spite of its biological and physical devastation, which give it an important world significance, with its creative fusion and original synthesis to promote its future. Such is the expression of its geological organic matter that its magmas have been a human melting pot.

Because of the geographical conception that it adopted, no one will be able to deny the archipelago of Cabo Verde a place and varied roles that after time has for example, led to Black Africa. **The dominance of world leadership will be determined by whomever controls the central land (Terra Central) or that which Mackinder called "the geographic axis of history**, *the archipelago of Cabo Verde"*, which will never be, given its magnificent position in the Atlantic and its current access to transoceanic communications, a marginal zone or being (in the meaning of Mackinder) simply an unused piece of land with an exterior that is crescent shaped and forgotten as an island group on that axis. An axis with so much to offer, making its way with ideas that translate and inspire, such as its special designation by an international organization victorious in World War II.

A dynamic center of convergence and diffusion, that is what the archipelago is all about and must be. **And as such it has its own outstanding features that we can mention. An admirable** *human experience, an unmistakable curious cultural personality, a multiracial society, that relies on happiness and a reserved suffering,* confused dreams of despair and of times gone by, mingled with a radiant dawn of hope.

But all of this is not just the result of its specific and uncontested geography. It is also the underlying and pervasive quality of its past, the shock and embrace of its social traditions with a profound and diverse history. Amid a thousand painful ups and downs, and so many cumbersome and immense difficulties, in the struggle against today's constant threats, whether age-old misfortunes or new ones, the colonization of Cabo Verde, and its present realities are simultaneously, the consequence of natural conditions and the action and reaction and the sentiment of men. They are really a panorama often tragically obscured, an admirable and fertile miracle of nature and of Portugal.

As we have already written, it is surprising how on these gloomy rocks of lava, generally a natural spectacle that is desolate, or even hostile, **often forgotten by the world**, while amid struggles and sufferings, the people can have good spirits, and work, dream and sing, that is, how they manage to survive and enjoy life. Well the grateful and triumphal reality is that what really happens, without which as we can see, it has become necessary to rely upon the fate of providence for the protection of the land and its people.

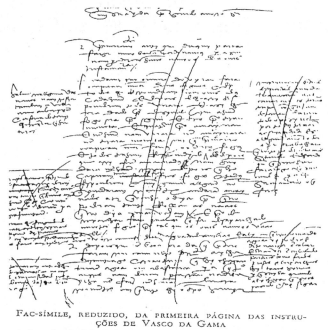

FAC-SÍMILE, REDUZIDO, DA PRIMEIRA PÁGINA DAS INSTRU-
ÇÕES DE VASCO DA GAMA

Leitura das 7 últimas linhas: Item depois que em boon ora daqui
partirem faram sscu caminho direito a ylha de Samtiago [d *mar-
gem:* se tornaram ante a ilha de sam nicolao no caso desta ne-
cesidade pela doença da ilha de sam tiago] e se ao tempo que
hy chegarem teucrem agoa em abastança pera quatro meses
nam deucm pousar na dita ylha nem fazer nenhuuma demora
ssoomente em quamto lhe o tempo servyr.

Vasco da Gama's Secret

This is the first page of a letter of instructions written by Vasco
da Gama after he returned from India, for Pedro Alvares
Cabral who was preparing to command the next voyage to
India at the end of 1499. In this letter (within the last seven
lines) da Gama advises Cabral to go straight to the island of
Sao Nicolau (also in Cabo Verde). It was during this voyage
that Cabral discovered Brazil, before continuing onward to
India in 1500, after departing from the Cape Verde islands.

Spanish Involvement in the Slave Trade in Cabo Verde- Map of Trade Route

In this section is shown very clearly that Spain was directly involved in the slave trade with Cabo Verde. we make the historic connection between Cabo Verde and the Hispanic world.

Reference: As Ilhas Afortunadas, 1986 by Basil Davidson, FCL

After 1600 many captives were taken from the continent and later sent to Brazil and the Caribbean, once they had undergone a period of 'training' in order that they become familiar with their new masters so that both master and slave could get to understand one another. In effect Cabo Verde served as a slave training school for new slaves and masters. In this way Cabo Verde became an intermediary slave station for the commercial slave trade in the Atlantic.

One example as cited by Antonio Carreira: "during the four years between 1609 and 1612, 1468 captives were offloaded on the island of Santiago, coming from the 'Rios de Cabo Verde' also known as the 'Rios da Guine' - another 8,110 slaves, already trained, were exported from Cabo Verde to Colombia Mexico, the Canary Islands and Seville in Spain".

Note: that these years were between 1581 and 1640 when Cabo Verde was part of Spain.

Then details taken directly from one of the documents that registered the transaction for the ship, 'Santo Antonio', on 20 December 1514, in which it says that on this date from the port of Ribeira Grande (S.Tiago-Cabo Verde), that the Spanish ship 'Santo Antonio' departed for Spain (Castille). Then it goes on to cite the names of the merchants and the number of slaves that were being purchased and their monetary value. For example, Christofo Nunez paid for eleven slaves of unequal value, that were appraised at 46,100 reis and among them were four small children. For this he paid a tax of 10% of the appraised value.

SLAVE TRADE ROUTES

SLAVE TRADE ROUTES

Slave ships departing Cabo Verde for Spain with details 1513-1515

This table shows the names of the ships, with the dates that they departed Cabo Verde and the number of slaves that were being shipped to Spain during the period 1513 - 1515.

SLAVE TRADE ROUTES - PORTUGAL-SPAIN-CABO VERDE-AFRICA

Exportation of slaves and hides (1513 – 1515)

Date of Departure	Name of Ship	Merchandise	
		Slaves	Hides
1513, 15 Dec	Madanela Cansina	139	308
1514, 6 June	Stª Maria	46	168
1514, 20 Dec	Santo Antonio	105	62
1515, 16 March	Santa Ana	82	
1515, 26 May	Maria de Golva	67	
1515, 7 August		37	
1515, 16 December	Stª Mª da Conceição	41	8
	Total	517	546

Details of slave ship "Santo Antonio" 1514

This statement is just a summary of some details of the slave trade based on a document dated 20 December 1514 and published in 'Historia general de Cabo Verde' by the Instituto de Investigação Cientifica Tropical – Lisbon 1990. First, it is important to state that the ship 'St Antonio' was a Spanish ship in the Port of Ribeira Grande and was departing for Spain (Castille). The merchants were being taxed by the tax collector for the following items:

Item: Gonçalo d Aça, the pilot of the ship was taxed for 6 slaves that were appraised at the minimum of 28,000 reais.
Taxed 10%   2,800 reais

Item: Pero Alonso and Afonso Alvarez were taxed for 10 slaves that were of unequal value and appraised at 50,063 reais.
Taxed 10%   5,063 reais

Item: Cristofo Nunez was taxed on 11 slaves of unequal value and appraised at 46,100 reais, because there were 4 small children in this group of 11, so a 10% tax of 4, 610 reais was levied.
Total taxes paid on this document was 12,473 reais (10% of 124,730-appraised value of slaves)

A document of 1493 registers the sale of a slave, about 18 years old, Diego from Jolofo (Guinea), from Goncalo of Cordova (Spain) to Francisco Lapidario of Seville (Spain).The price of the purchase is also registered in this document -9,000 maravedies.

2 Jul 1493
Archivo de Protocolos de Sevilla
Escrituras del Siglo XV, Oficio XII
Registo notarial da venda de Diego, escravo negro, de cerca de 18 anos, natural de Jolof (Jalofo).*
Ano de 1493 - Martes 2 de julio.= Vende Goncalo de Cordova, vezino de la
dicha cibdad de Cordova, a Francisco Lapidario, vezino de esta cibdad de Sevilla
en la collacion de Saint Ysidro, que está presente, un esclavo de color negro que ha nonbre
Diego de hedad de dies e ocho anos poco mas o menos, natural de Jolof... por
prescio de nueve mill maravedies, que otorga los rescibio, y son en su poder.

*We should note that Jalofo is in Guine and was under the administative control of Cabo Verde and that the Spanish did not have the right to practice commerce in this territory and normally would have had to negotiate with Portugal in order to purchase slaves from Guine which would be acquired in the Cape Verde Islands.

VOLUME III

The 'Missing Pages of Blacks and Hispanics in history

EXAMPLES OF ATROCITIES THAT CONFIRM OUR HISTORY

The Extermination of Cabo Verde (Frightening Revelations) by Luis Loff de Vasconcellos 1903 - Lisbon - An unpublished text

This is a reminder to all of the emigrants of the Cape Verdean Diaspora scattered around the world and to all those emigrants who came from Europe and received assistance from Cape Verdeans while enroute to South America, South Africa and Australia, without ever being aware of the consequences and suffering of the cape verdean people.

This special reminder is also dedicated to the descendants of all of these emigrants with the hope that they will come to learn about the history and the contributions made by the Cape Verdean people. Most of these people are totally unaware of this impact on their lives.

For the reader of this book, I wanted to include some essays by contemporary writers during the harsh times in Cabo Verde. In this way, those emigrants and their dependents who represent the Diaspora of Cabo Verde will become aware of their past. Since there is a lot of xenophobia in the world today due to racism, I wanted to show the world that in Cabo Verde the people had to suffer together in spite of their ethnicity, but always as Cape Verdeans. The people of these islands are united by history as one group of people in spite of their ethnic differences. For this reason, others find it difficult to understand the unity of this society. In those countries where the government imposes racial categories upon their citizens to divide their budgets according to race it becomes a great controversy in the case of Cape Verdeans. In this situation Cape Verdeans are unique in the history of mankind and their adhesion is the result of the Age of Discoveries and more than 500 years existing as a new type of person according to modern anthropologists. In this sense I hope that the descendants of Cape Verdeans can understand their history and maintain this adhesion as homage to their ancestors.

146

For those governments that wish to classify people by their racial characteristics or by other ignorant means, they are going to destroy the cape verdean families (and perhaps other groups as well) without any conscience whatsoever.

This is the truth, especially in Cape Verdean communities, which already have a history of intense racial integration for more than five centuries.

The Cape Verdean community is a brotherhood with a long history that can serve as a model for other societies concerned about the race based xenophobia that exists today.

In Cabo Verde there has already passed a long history of the glory and the suffering amongst everyone, Africans, Europeans, Arabs, Jews, Asians, Indians and mestizos.

Still a few more details about these sufferings. These essays were written during the early part of the 20th century when many Cape Verdeans where going to the United States and today the children and grandchildren of these pioneers are unaware of their history, because there aren't any publications available to the general public (in schools, libraries, bookstores, etc.) to confirm this history.

The history of this suffering is painful and difficult, but I also believe that the world must become aware of the past in order to improve upon the future.

The following information is taken from a text by Luis L. Vasconcellos which shows several letters written to him by friends of his in describing the conditions of the famine of 1903 on Santiago. Vasconcellos was a lawyer in Cabo Verde and served as the Director of the Meteorological Department on the island of San Vicente. He is also credited with being one of the more important writers whose works contributed to the Independence of Cabo Verde which finally arrived in 1975. He certainly was a distinguished civil rights leader during his time, in the late 1800's and early 1900's. In one of his more direct comments he wrote, "many people on the continent (Portugal) seem to imagine that our African colonies, are occupied by blacks and savages, and that everyone born here is black and savage. That is a grave mistake. There are in many African colonies, especially in Cabo Verde a large number of natural Portuguese, remote descendants or recent descendants of Europeans, who are in no way inferior to the native born Portuguese of the continent." He also spoke of the unity of the Cape Verdean people and the unnecessary suffering that they endured. He was also very familiar with the situation in Africa and wrote extensively about the treatment of the people in Guine. I hope that one day a detailed study will be made of his writings, so the world will know that everyone was not silent during the period of suffering in Cabo Verde. And yes, people who believe in justice can make a difference.

DREADFUL REVELATIONS

Luis Loff Vasconcellos 1903

The fearful and horrifying catastrophe for which our overseas brethren are being the victims - the poor Cape Verdeans - a newspaper campaign has recently begun in this capital to express the sincere recognition of the suffering of the Cape Verdean people with dignity and words of praise.

A reaching out for compassion and mercy is being reflected in this capital, arousing altruistic sentiments in the hearts of the generous and in the souls of the philanthropists and well wishers, who are seeking solutions and finding relief for the thousands of the unfortunate who are at this very moment suffering from the horrors of starvation on what used to be a rich island of abundance; Santiago, in Cabo Verde.

At the head of this charitable movement, we have the goodwill Commercial Association of Lisbon, already collecting important donations from the generous merchants of this city, having left some days ago for Cabo Verde with a portion of the contributions, that certainly will save hundreds of creatures from the claws of death, because without this assistance it appears inevitable that they will die of starvation.

Associations like these, know that by their influence, they can avail themselves to a noble and just cause and being inspirational in the purest sentiments of patriotism and charity.

The Commercial Association of Lisbon has just revealed to the country that it is not just honoring its mission, but is also showing that it is a useful corporation that is generous and benefiting the suffering.

Thus leaving an indelible imprint on the hearts of the cape verdean people with this act of goodwill.

But on behalf of the government, there is still much to be done, because little, in fact, very little has been done so far.

They say that they are trying to find ways to reach these thousands of unfortunates, who are begging for help and are dying by the dozens on a daily basis, by a cruel and pitiful agony; but up until now, still can not find the means or at least, not those that are controlled by the state, that is being expected with great anxiety to put an end to this deviating slaughter, that is destroying many cape verdeans on the island of Santiago.

This is a very dangerous responsibility that the government has assumed, before the nation, continuing this situation of relief while thousands of Portuguese subjects in a Portuguese colony are allowed to die of starvation.

This is the ultimate annihilation of the people.

It is ridiculous and cynical the argument, to say that the government press is providing help, and that the government is not the blame because it does not rain.

The Cape Verdean people on Santiago are dying and it is due to the lack of receiving timely provisions.

With just half the effort that they are now making, there wouldn't have to be a single death by starvation.

But no; **The population of Santiago is dying of hunger and this is causing it to disappear, because the vote has been taken for extermination.**

About three thousand emigrants to different locations, have already abandoned the islands of Cabo Verde; **nearly one thousand hunger deaths are already lying in open grave sites**, in the cemeteries and in the fields.

What else is there?

A shabby hungry population suffering in a state of starvation, that is succumbing to the horrors of famine, a flight of misery and already do not have the strength to beg for food. A cycle of terrible famine that is killing nearly 80 people per day. And everything is available in the coffers of the provisional resources, to extinguish this evil punishment. Still not long ago there must have been about 400,000 reis (monetary unit) available. That's right; 400,000 reis, and this is money for the people, yet they are allowed to die of hunger. This is a crime, that is of the most hateful and repugnant kind imaginable that is happening in this colony!

This is the extermination of the people and a people that has always been a loyal ally of the mother land. This is annihilating the province of Cabo Verde; reducing it to torture , with a stack of bodies over a vast desolate terrain.

When God sprays water on these fields that would bring an abundance of crops, there will not be any hands available to plant the seeds: they will be eaten by the worms at the bottom of their graves, or far away in distant lands, cultivating the fields in some foreign country while those in their motherland shall remain barren and uncultivated.

Unfortunately this is the situation in which Cabo Verde is condemned; basically, a burning volcano that is swallowing up lives. One can see this frightening situation very clearly, this grim disaster that is bringing terror and death to thousands of our unfortunate brethren. This is a war of extermination against a defenseless people that has been humiliated in spite of its dignity; it is a revolting villain and an indescribable monstrosity and a crime against humanity declared on the cape verdean people by the government, and which we are now exposing to the country and to the press, appealing to the noble sentiments of the Portuguese people and the national press (of Portugal), so that an energetic and general movement will be made and to sound the alarms once more, on behalf of the people who are suffering, a people who are dying of hunger and begging for charity and donations.

And still: they demand responsibility and require the examination of all the facts, so that communications will be published daily in Cabo Verde in the various newspapers, with full disclosures in order to shed light on this matter.

The country can not sit around with its arms folded in front of this embarrassing sacrifice, nor can it become through its silence, in solidarity with it. There are hundreds of foreigners passing through Cabo Verde who are getting the impression that we are a bunch of cannibals (1903). Our disgrace as a colonial nation is already terrifying, and so there is a need to substantiate the facts that actually exist in Cabo Verde, which will fully justify it.

As we have seen before, with the private charity, when the press sounds the first alarm, then the action starts, during this period outside help starts heading for Cabo Verde, two hundred sacks of general provisions, gathered by open contributions by the Commercial Association of Lisbon.

Now it is urgent that the government dispense with customs duties, and start facing the frightening crisis that is killing 70 - 80 people per day in Santiago.

To throw dust in the eyes of the public and to calm the press, the government has made the most of a telegram written by the governor of Cabo Verde that says:

151

"I am distributing rations two times per day to the needy from the interior, who number about 1,500 here in the city (Praia). I have distributed to the needy in three places, at the edge of the plateau of the city. I distributed a half liter of milk for each child, who numbered about 100, they also have medical assistance.

I am also sheltering many woman and children.

The provisional lodging for men and woman are the best that is possible.

I'm ordering the construction of new shelters.

I've directed that 1,000 people be given work on the road to Picos.

However, despite a shortage of men, many prefer to beg in the city.

I've employed 450 people on the farm lands.

In the beginning of August we'll start to repair the roads to the Old City (Cidade Velha) and the road to Orgaos, on the island of Santiago.

I have resources for all of these authorizations.

Yours Truly, the Governor"

Now, according to the text of this telegram, it appears that the complaints that were made by the press were false and unfounded. Everything appears to have been provided. The hungry have the best shelters possible, the children have milk, 1,000 workers have been employed on the roads to Picos, and so far there is plenty of work for many men and in fact there is a shortage of men for jobs, and these men prefer to beg in the city and the governor has the resources for all the ministerial authorizations.

That telegram had been sent from Praia (the capital city) on the 14th of this current month of July, on the same day that the steam ship 'Cabo Verde' departed Praia for Lisbon and arrived there on the 21st.

152

Do you really want to know the truth about the situation as it actually existed on the 14th of July? Then read the following correspondence by our dear friend who is beyond suspicion and fully trustworthy.

THE FAMINE ON THE ISLAND OF SANTIAGO

The city of Praia, 14 July 1903.

• The famine on the island of Santiago has reached its peak. Some are still having their doubts about it, whether because of their perversity or their refusal to look as they turn their heads in front of the horrible spectacle that presents its ugly head every day; others, full of guilt, are perhaps beating their chests and saying penance.

• Practical men of good judgment have foreseen that which is now happening here in the province. That is the lack of help and support at the right time, which could have prevented this great massacre.

• The hospital is already filled and doesn't have space to take in any more patients, as they are carried on stretchers or in the arms of the police, and this in spite of the fact that for very 10 that enter, there are 6 or 7 who will be buried in the cemetery on the following day. Outside of the hospital there is a private home that is being operated as an infirmary just for children, who have been roaming around abandoned, sick and anemic, by the hundreds, and they say that another is going to open up.

• Another warehouse of the Department of Public Works is being used to shelter the people who have been coming in from the interior and were living in the streets in the suburbs of the city, but the wandering population is over 2,000 people.

• In the cemetery they have opened up ditches as open grave sites to bury the dead and in the rural parishes (districts), some cemeteries no longer take in any more bodies.

- You can estimate that the mortality effected by the famine in the city of Praia and vicinity in the month of June to be about 160 people. On the island today the death rate must be reaching about 70 - 80 per day and this number is expected to increase until the end of the month and start to include larger numbers when the first rains start, then an enormous number of people who were roaming around dying and without shelter will certainly die due to the despair in which they will find themselves.
- The situation is critical and the impediments to curtail the crisis today are greater, we are the first to confess to that; but the precautionary arrangements are insufficient and the work on the road to Picos in the center of the island is being reduced, they can't help thousands of men.
- The situation is terrible, in a state that has left its people, in difficulties to regulate long term assistance, when they determine it to be necessary, it will be tremendous, because there is nothing set up to give serious study to this matter.
- A private initiative can do a lot, but it's necessary that the famine doesn't cover the whole island.
- There would be many necessities to set up, welfare assistance programs in the different parishes, but these programs would have to be designated by the governor, in order to make a certain impression of authority, so that donors could be solicited, setting up economical soup lines and managing them, while keeping the government informed about their progress and to avoid emigration to other parts of the island, where they (the needy) would be without shelter and establishing a crowd of people, thus provoking more inconvenience in the current struggle.
- These and other precautionary measures will have to be taken.
- The council administrator of Praia is tired and overworked by all the services due to the famine, a commission in the capital would alleviate that authority, which has a lot to do with the making of this situation.

- With the mass influx of people coming to the capital from various parts of the island, the public health is threatened, as these people are living on the outskirts of the capital, under the worst type of misery and filth that one can imagine.
- The human waste of these people will cause a foul odor, which emanates from the rocks that are becoming sensitive to the pressing heat.
- The famine with all of its horrors are decimating the people of Santiago.
- Already this appeal is not just for the government of Portugal; this appeal is for the whole country, requesting help and charitable support for those people who are starving to death on the doorsteps of the motherland.
- So why then, if so many precautionary measures have been taken, are there 80 people dying this very day from hunger?
- There is shelter for everyone and yet in the streets of the suburbs of the city there are 2,000 people?
- And here is still another letter from a friend of ours, dated 15 July, from Sao Vicente:

Dear Luis,
Cabo Verde is no longer a Portuguese colony. What I have just heard from Costa and Nosolini, who today left for Lisbon, is frightening. There are more than 50 people dying daily on the island of Santiago, dying of starvation, and this has been verified by doctors with death certificates!!!
Costa tells me that he is coming across dead bodies all the time on the streets of the city. I won't say any more now because the steam ship is ready to leave. An interview with the son of our friend, Antonio Pedro Costa, who went with Nosolini today, knows very well the horrors. The newspaper is giving it publicity, but to mean anything; it must be in the name of humanity."
Well, how can you explain these facts, after reading the telegram that the governor sent and up to a point has cooled down the campaign? Is the telegram correct or is our information false? One can not hide from this

dilemma. But, before the nation can make a statement on this matter, we still have more information to pursue, from a person in whom we have confidence, also written on the 14th of July from the city of Praia:

'What I have heard and witnessed in this city, is truly hair raising, as I arrive, I do not understand and have no doubt what my eyes are seeing, because incredibly it is happening in this century in a nation such as ours that is proud of its humanitarianism, and apparently such a nation would intentionally wish death upon its citizens.

It is truly a war of extermination against the Cape Verdean people. They would like that this day be absolutely tested, the complete extinction of this race, they want that Cabo Verde be deserted. That is a sad system of colonization, just for cannibals.

I am not sure just what the provincial governor has reported to the minister, however, what is taken for granted by those who always accompany the governor and go against the cape verdean people and who do not make false pretenses in stating that they must disappear (the Cape Verdean people), these say that the governor has requested precautionary measures regarding assistance, but the minister says that there is nothing to do but to let them die!

In the telegraph the blame was established and not any telegram that is sent can describe the famine or those who have died. There are at least 12 a day dying just in the capital alone, right in front of the authorities, this is an uncontested fact. There are hundreds of skinny, filthy and shabby people, suffering from the famine, who are coming from the interior daily and begging to the authorities and they are ignored and permitted to die. What does this mean?

When these wretched souls are dying, we send them to the hospital, where soon afterwards they take their last breath. There they are pronounced dead and the doctor completes the appropriate certificate 'Death by Starvation'. Well, the enemies of the state are indignant to all that. Isn't this enough to prove that they would wish death to these unfortunate people? This is

156

undoubtedly unbelievable, because **no one can imagine the scene of this horror**. But the government is inclined to have absolute certainty that this is the expression of the truth. And still it is indispensable to send someone, energetic, intelligent, and serious, to know the truth. **The truth of this picture is truly horrifying**. A commission should be sent, that includes a doctor, to hear and see just exactly what is going on, and learn the truth; i.e., that in Cabo Verde, they are committing the worst possible crime against humanity, which has not been seen, since the days of old Rome.

But this can be a continuing problem, that Portugal, the old Portugal, country of chivalry, the first to end slavery, and now in this century they want to demonstrate in front of the whole world, that in the end, that they are more savage than even the savages themselves!!

Denying food to a dying people right in front of our very eyes and still using methods, that are unknown abroad, something so appalling that they will tell all the people of Europe: that it is a lie! But ask all of those who come to Cabo Verde. Send them to the government, people of absolute confidence and independent, serious and honest people, and you will know that this still represents the truth.

In Cabo Verde, they are telling us that everything that you have just read is absolutely atrocious.

I still have to clarify a point in the famous telegram. That is where it says: many men are needed for work, but they prefer to beg in the city. Concerning this statement, someone who arrived in Cabo Verde on the last steam ship, writes:

'The people of Cabo Verde are workers, having hunger is not believed to deny work and actually it doesn't deny it, I guarantee it. Those who are refusing work in Picos and prefer to beg in Praia are those who have families living 7 to 8 leagues away (approximately 35 to 40 k's or 22 to 25 miles). Can a woman with 2, 3, or 4 children be expected to leave them at home (with whom?), to go and earn 40 or 60 reis (old Portuguese coins) 7 leagues from home?

Here's your answer:

Who will take them to Picos? From where will they come? Who will provide shelter? There's still more: the person is hungry begging for food: and is expected to go to Picos. There goes someone dragging their frail body 7 leagues. Upon arrival asking for food! - FIRST WORK AND THEN YOU SHALL BE FED!! And this person will have to work a week with hunger in order to receive 8 patacos (old Portuguese copper coin) afterwards (or something of equivalent value) while going to work on time, and providing nourishment to a starving woman and children?

And this still isn't anything. Some show up who want to go to Picos, or perhaps they do not have any family responsibilities and have a place to stay and make it to Picos. And upon arrival are told: Sorry, no more work available. Returning to Praia, pleading for public assistance and are told: What you scoundrels want, is this! Go to Picos!

But, sir...

Go away scoundrel.

...I went to Picos...

Sure, but you didn't want to work. You'd rather beg for charity. Go! Go!

...and they didn't give me work.

I've already told you, go away.

And they tell them that they are hungry!

Also, now we don't believe that the hungry of Cabo Verde are being denied work, so that they may beg, allowing themselves to die senselessly, while the government is as it pretends to make one believe, that it is prepared to give work for food.

No one can really believe in facts like these.

Cabo Verde would have to be a land of the rich and well off, so that the habitual begging would liberate the miserable indigenous people who are roaming the streets of the city and the roads in the interior of the island, like mummies.

No; if there is anything positive about the truth it is this: the government only gives them food when they are not able to work anymore and are unable to feed themselves.

The people of Cabo Verde have been slandered by the epithet that they are lazy and imprudent, and also when there is a regular rainfall, neither are they without, the magnates, their slanderers, to cultivate the fields, nor who give them bread.

We see here on the European continent, that when a factory is closed that paralyzes an industry, they launch a deafening campaign screaming out; 20,000 workers dying of hunger!

Where then, is the concern of the continental people?

But what is bad is yet something else. Those who earn just enough for their daily food, have nothing left to put away in storage.

This storage of food supplies is available only to those who exploit the labor of the people, or those who receive resources and benefits from the government.

The people of Cabo Verde are dying of hunger. This is what the telegram of the governor of Cabo Verde should have disclosed to the nation, it is this which must be said; but no, with respect to this ghastly catastrophe, not one single word - because the truth is, this would establish serious responsibilities for a government that is inhumane and barbaric.

The number of victims is tremendous. It is horrifying, that which is happening in Cabo Verde! Here is what one eye witness has told us:

'Bands of miserable, shabby and bony people are attacking pedestrians and begging for help; women with children on their backs, on their laps and or in their hands, they look like death, repugnant , and covered with scabies and filth, eyes gazing outward, crying out in monotonous tones; I'm hungry! I'm hungry! The older ones use a cane (stick), dragging it with difficulty, begging for charity, all over the city, the same desolate spectacle, the same terrifying misery. In front of some homes, groups of vagabonds sit in front of the walkway. They are awaiting an old lady with eyes staring out and a mouth wide open, the chest gasping for air and with difficulty breathing, who will be interrupted by the habitual begging.

159

We are visiting a large shed where they are distributing the so called 'economic soup' and we have seen women and children, about 200 people in the same miserable condition. A crude meal, poorly cooked, that might satisfy adults, but for the old and sick people, and children, it is repulsive. Only one ration of soup by the government is distributed at a cost of 26 reis each. The price defies description and commentaries. Still, there was approval for more than 500 candidates, who were being served in simple clay bowls, filled to capacity so that they would avoid the intense rays of the sun, they were expected to spread out on the floor, in a disorderly shapeless mass, scratching scabies, sores and vermin, that would disturb them during the meal distribution process, that they craved. Once this started, they often trampled over one another to be served, in the midst of an indescribable confusion with sinister screams and fear.

In the bowls, they received a little bit of boiled corn, that they ate with their hands or directly, like pigs in a pigpen. During this distribution, the only spectacle that was consoling was the police who were full of patience, attending to so many unfortunates without violence.'

But our news does not stop here, concerning the flagrant telegram with which we disagree.

There is one more here, signed by the correspondent himself. Note carefully the date, which is one day before the telegram from Cabo Verde.

FAMINE IN CABO VERDE

Praia, 13 July 1903.

In one of the latest sessions of parliament, Mr. Dantes Baracho demanded a statement from the minister about the famine that is decimating Cabo Verde.

Mr. Hintze Ribeiro, president of the council of ministers who was present, declared that the crisis was caused by the measures taken by the government, ordering the expansion of public works, establishing economic soup lines and reducing entitlements for corn.

160

But the practice of these arrangements didn't get here, for the reason that the public works didn't expand but very succinctly and the economic soups became aggravated by the distribution and much less indignant of that which they demanded (only one ration of soup per day) and as a consequence of this bad orientation is the fact they are dying of starvation, a colony that is 5 days travel from the capital of the kingdom, and from the gates of Europe, hundreds of people that could be examined by doctors! The scene of the city is causing fear by seeing the unfortunate starving all over the streets and begging for public charity.

Thousands of the hungry have become invalids due to the famine and can no longer work nor can they count on any resources, and they can only wait for the next harvest, about four months from now (if God sends rain), these will have to be victims, because there won't be enough resources for them, whether for jobs or for charitable donations.

Unfortunately we have to help this sad staff and guard against a new crisis for next year, because a large portion of the land must remain uncultivated for lack of labor and the lack of resources; everything that was caused by the cruel and criminal administrative orientation, exercised by the first officials in whom they confided, who are determining the fate of this province, those who seem to want to see the complete annihilation and destruction of this ill-fated colony.

In summary, everything should be released that would be necessary to reach these unfortunate people, who are told that public funds are not always applied by the best standards, and amazingly , sometimes, undeserved gratification's go to close affiliations (friends). I'm ending for today and until the next time, we remain.

Yours truly,

Manuel Romano de Mello

In this correspondence it can be said that the economic soup being distributed is a mockery of the system and much less indignant of that which is the reality, and only one serving per day.

And the telegram said: "I'm distributing rations twice a day to the needy."

Where is the truth?

What we already know based on the available facts, is that it is a long way from the reality of what Mr. Ribeiro declared: "that the crisis is being averted by the precautions taken by the government".

This is truly unbelievable, everything that is happening with respect to Cabo Verde. This is taking place in a country that is fostering obscurity and denial of the truth, while permitting thousands of its people to die of starvation.

In order to see the state of disgrace that has come to the province of Cabo Verde and the way that it has been abandoned by the leadership of the authorities, we are transcribing a passage of a letter of one of our friends from San Vicente.

NEWS:

Fifteen days ago, a man from the island of Santo Antao, by the name of Gilberto, wound up as a prisoner by order of the administration of the council, and yesterday he was being sent to Praia, they say, for the purpose of being sent to S. Tome. (Sao Tome, it should be noted, was a group of islands where people were sent by the government to work on sugar cane plantations. Today it is an independent country like Cabo Verde and there is a large colony of Cape Verdeans living there, mainly as a result of this type of emigration. There are two main islands S. Tome and Principe which are located off the south western coast of Africa in the vicinity of Angola).

The man, however had by his side some four to six fellow countrymen, managing demands for the judge, showing him; a family man, who hadn't committed any crime whatsoever, without being blamed for anything and without due process; that he would be exiled. (Here I think it is important to note that the Portuguese word 'degradado' is used in the Portuguese text, and this is in reference to those subjects who were often considered to be criminals, who would be sent to (exiled to) colonial provinces such as Cabo Verde or Brazil to provide local labor and increase the population of these areas and as has been stated above, many Cape Verdeans were sent to S. Tome to provide labor. Was this a voluntary process or a

162

forced labor process, resembling slavery? It appears that much of this labor was involuntary based upon the information that I have reviewed.)

The judge, being dignified and straightforward, ordered the prisoner to appear before him at 3.00 P.M. and in this case the exile order was avoided, but the man went back to prison and today there are new requests, that were being reviewed by the M.P., but as of this moment I know nothing more.

What deserves particular attention on the part of those who are interested in public freedom is the act of the same administrator who had ordered a hand paddling (flogging of the palm of the hand with a flat stick) and which was to be carried out at the entrance hall of the administration of the council, and those to be castigated would be prostitutes or men found in violation of any offense. These were ordered to be detained in the referenced hall and informed that when the judge of the court retires he meets with 3 or 4 policemen who approach the accused one by one in his presence, applying the hand paddling in the midst of cries and tears, etc.

Some days ago someone told me that one more bold person said he would refuse his hand and said, that the first person to touch it would get his head smashed, then it would be the administrator, and then this one would willingly have his hand flogged!!

Cabo Verde has regressed 50 years or more and these examples are terrifying for its future. **The people are going to feel persecuted**,* and should these scenes be repeated at another time with so many deaths, the authorities will not be surprised.

*I found this to be a very interesting statement, in considering the situation of the American Cape Verdeans, many of them who came to America during this period or shortly thereafter.

Many of the descendants of American Cape Verdeans have had great difficulty in trying to understand their parents and grandparents. It seems as though they were always shrouded by a great wall of silence, a mysterious behavior that seems to have been the result of some strange form of persecution in their past. And certainly there would be more famines and more deaths resulting from starvation in Cabo Verde as the author predicted above. So it should not surprise anyone who

163

knows an American Cape Verdean to discover that these people have often lived with a persecution complex in America, where people are generally polarized along black and white lines, thus effectively closing the door in the face of many Cape Verdeans who are a multicultural people who have suffered together throughout their history. Hopefully, that by disclosing information of this nature for the first time in history Americans will have the opportunity to better understand the American Cape Verdean as well as the Europeans in Europe who encounter Cape Verdeans, or for that matter, anyone who encounters Cape Verdeans anywhere in the world, because this was a problem that until now has not really been exposed before.

And what does the government have to say about this?

- What kind of regime do we have here?
- Well, we can say that there isn't any civilized colony that administers corporal punishment as does Cabo Verde?
- Is this a disgraceful situation?
- And it is surely for this that the government is contracting 15 guards here for S. Vicente, with the fabulous earnings of 1,500 reis per day, earnings superior to that of most department heads in this province.
- Fifteen guards in S. Vicente at a cost of 675,000 reis per month, when the service that is being rendered there is excellent for the country's guards and they are earning only 400 reis (per day), that says it all!
- And this, just at the moment that the country is going backwards, a horrible scene and at a time when the people are starving to death!
- Why is it necessary to have such expensive guards in a land where the people are still being castigated by hand paddling (palmatorias) like a five year old kid?
- For all that has been exposed here, one can see that Cabo Verde is coming to its final moments of the extermination and its moral decomposition and only by a supernatural power will it be able to rise up from the bottom of this abyss.

• A half a dozen charlatans are there who brag about the importance and wisdom, that are connected with the 'mata-pretos'; those who are being hand paddled, and no one speaks out because they are wickedly hovering above this unprotected land, a frightening spectrum of famine that is harvesting the lives and destroying their courage and energy, and even those who happen to have capital; the despots and those oppressed by law, and not one cynical smile to condemn the maltreatment of these people and they rely on impunity.

• What else is there to do? To ask compassion for a humble and starving people. And we who never ask for mercy from anyone, now we must ask it for our brothers in Cabo Verde.

• Heavens forbid!

• We close this letter, as we are reading in the newspapers yet another telegram from the governor of Cabo Verde, dated 22 July, which says:

"I have arrived in the interior where I want to organize the distribution of rations to the destitute in the villages of the parishes of S, Miguel, Orgaos, S. Tiago and Picos. I bought 260,000 liters of corn to sustain the hungry. The construction of the road in Cidade Velha is to begin on the 25th of this month. The road to Orgaos will be impossible to start before the 1st of August. The road to Picos has employed 1,200 people, there is a shortage of 400 men who are poorly substituted by women and boys. The government is currently feeding 1,800 people in the city of Praia, I'll make a report on everything the next time."

• Another slap in the face for the public by the government.

• They say that there is a shortage of 400 men on the road to Picos, and they are being poorly substituted by women and boys.

• Just what are they trying to say here? There will be a shortage of 400 men; that they are being poorly substituted?

165

- That there aren't any more people to work in Cabo Verde?
- But, on the 25th they are going to open up new jobs on the road to Cidade Velha and on the 1st of August, on the road to Orgaos, when there aren't any men to work.
- We think that in this part, the telegram would have been better off if it read: in the region of Picos, he already gave work to 1,200 people, all of them, having had valid requirements.
- The number of starving on the whole island of Santiago is estimated to be; without exaggeration; about 15,000 people.
- The poverty-stricken are spread out in different areas on the island of Santiago which measures about 18 leagues (90 k's or 60 miles) in length and anyone who knows Cabo Verde can understand the reason why there would be a 400 man shortage in Picos for work.
- And the rest of the needy, already do not have the strength to get themselves up to there, where the governor had up until now centralized all the work.
- Picos is about 6 to 8 leagues (30 to 40 k's or 20 to 25 miles) away from the points where the number of hungry are the greatest, considering that this distance would have to be covered on foot, since Cabo Verde, thanks to the development that the governor has provided, still does not have even the pleasure of steamship transportation.
- Still, that part of the telegram that says the government is feeding 1,800 of the needy in Praia, can only appease those who don't know that the number of starving in Praia has reached 3,000.
- But, it is possible that now the grants coming to Cabo Verde will increase the number of rations.
- It is also still possible that these 3,000 needy people will die of indigestion! Such a case would not be unknown to science.

- We close by asking the national press one more time, that the holy crusade request for aid be continued for the hungry of Cabo Verde and to petition the governor to take speedy and efficient measures to put an end to this horrible situation.
- Lisbon, 25 July 1903.

Note: It is obvious that the revelations of the information above should have been known and exposed before, but I suspect, one of the difficulties would have been the fact that, in spite of everything, the traditional Cape Verdean was always proud to be Cape Verdean and loyal to Portugal as was seen in the works of Colonel Couto Ribeira Villas. And perhaps the people actually believed that this famine was the direct result of nature as they were being told and thus did not have the available facts which are cited in these writings. Besides if you are poor and starving to death how would you really know the truth, in a system where the truth was obscured?

Did the Cape Verdeans abroad know the details of this text? It does not appear to be so, because this was during a period when many Cape Verdeans were contracted to work for American companies on whaling boats and eventually settling in America. It should also be noted that the men who became whalers came from the interior of the islands and among those who were suffering the most and anyone who has ever read the novel 'Moby Dick' by Herman Melville, knows that it takes a lot of courage to be a whaler and that these were not lazy people. Their concerns would have naturally been to help their family and friends emigrate to America, which is what they did in fact do, once they were financially able to do so. Nevertheless, it seems that the traumatic experiences that are included in these essays above, must have left a devastating imprint on the minds of these pioneers in America, while making it extremely difficult if not impossible to pass this information down to their children. Was it embarrassment or was it fear? Only God can answer that. But, certainly many of them suffered. It becomes even more humiliating when these people find discrimination in their daily lives in their new homes abroad whether in America or Europe and people, or the system try to separate them by ethnicity. This of course, would be incomprehensible to the vast majority of them.

How can you concentrate on race when you have so many other problems trying to survive?

When genocide is mentioned everyone screams and the world eventually takes notice. But in traditional cases of genocide, there is always someone to blame for the horrors and there is usually killing with machetes or guns or some other instrument of death such as gas ovens, but, as was seen in the above essays, nowhere is it found in the history of mankind that God is blamed, when clearly it was man himself who committed the crimes which were effectively deflected to God.

After nearly a hundred years the truth has been hidden in history, because after all who could imagine that this could happen in a civilized country that was proud of its humanitarianism. This has been one of the great puzzles in the history of the Cape Verdean people, and although the issue has been raised in the past, there never seemed to be any answers available before now.

The closest example that I can think of today would be the case of Montserrat, the island in the Caribbean, where a volcano erupted recently in the summer of 1997, and Great Britain was accused by the natives of the island of not doing enough for the islanders , who are British subjects. The attitude of the British as reported in the media, appears to have been that there isn't much to be done against the evils of nature (God) and the government will provide standby transportation for them to leave if they desire to do so.

The islanders themselves have complained that this wasn't the attitude when the Falkland Islands requested assistance in their time of need. It presents a very curious study of human nature that needs to be documented as well as resolved. I'm sure that there are many who have their suspicions as to what the underlying causes of such indifference are in these cases. However, it takes courage to speak out, but unfortunately, those who do speak are often those to whom no one seems to listen or even want to hear.

There is hope, because of modern technology, there are many possibilities for people to work together around the globe to attempt to understand the problems of the voiceless, while taking actions that are constructive, which contribute to solutions. Believe it or not we are all in this together and it is time that we understand this crucial point at a crucial point in history on the eve of the next millennium.

MEMORIES OF A CAPE COD
CAPE VERDEAN COMMUNITY

Louis (LuLu) Babbitt

The best thing that someone can say about you, is that you respected people and was there and willing to help at anytime and anywhere. I find that there are very few Cape Cod Cape Verdeans who are not like that.

Ships used for commerce,e.g. slaves (water color)

THE COLUMBUS MAP

La Carta de Cristóbal Colón, Mapamundi, 1492

This is the map attributed to Columbus, who it is believed by historians to have personally made the map and written in the commentaries. Next to the Cape Verde Islands Columbus wrote a paragraph about the discovery of the islands. The inscription is written in Latin and reads:

«Hec insule vocantur italico sermone Cavo Verde, latino vero Promontorium Viride, que invente sunt quodan genuense cuis nomen erat Anthonius de Noli, a quo ispse insule denominante sunt et nomen adhuc retinent inventoris.»

171

English Translation:
«This island that we call Cavo Verde (Cabo Verde) was discovered by the Genoese Antonio da Noli and thus it was named after the discoverer and this name has been retained and used even today»

Portuguese Translation:
«Esta ilha chamados Cabo Verde que foi descoberta pelo genovese Antonio da Noli, e assim foi nomeada, até hoje se conserva o nome do descobridor.»

This information is extremely important as it confirms that Columbus was well aware of Antonio da Noli and his discovery of Cabo Verde. I'm also well aware that some historians have doubts about the accuracy of the authorship of this map.

In order to satisfy my own judgement on this matter I spoke with Dr Jose Luis Comellas a professor at the famous university in Seville, Spain who is recognized internationally as an expert on Columbus. He told me that he examined all the details on this map and that he was certain without a doubt that the work was made by Columbus based on many details that can only be found in works that have been personally made by Columbus. Thus we have here for perhaps the first time in history a direct connection between Columbus and Antonio da Noli. A connection that can easily be verified by studying the details on the map made by Juan de la Cosas in 1500 which is also displayed in this book.

THE MAP BY JUAN DE LA COSA

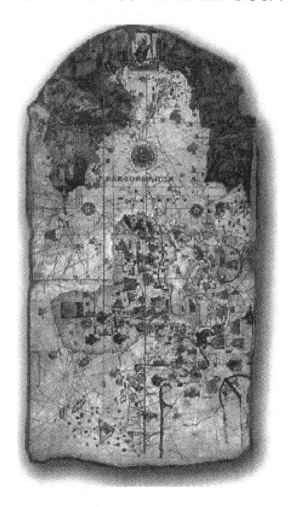

This map was made by an officer who sailed on the Santa Maria and accompanied Columbus on his first voyage across the Atlantic. Next to the Cape Verde Islands is the inscription: "Ilha de Antonio" (Antonio's Island) ou del Cavo Verde (or Cabo Verde). This is testimony to the fact that Columbus' crew was well aware of Antonio da Noli and Cabo Verde (The Cape Verde Islands).

173

INTERNATIONAL CAPE VERDEAN ORGANIZATIONS

ARGENTINA
- Associação Cultural e Recreativa

A/C Consulado Honorario de Cabo Verde, Montevideo 602, Bernal PCIA, Buenos Aires, Argentina
- Associação Cultural e Desportiva Cabo-Verdiana

Calle Moreno 118, Ensenada, Provincia de Buenos Aires, Argentina
- Uniaõ Cabo Verdiana

Leando N. Alem 1468, C.C. Dock Sud, Avellandeda (codigo 1871), Argentina

ANGOLA
- Associação Cabo-verdiana

A/C da Embaixada de Cabo Verde em Angola, Rua Alexandre Peres 29, 1° Luanda, Republica Popular de Angola

BRASIL
- Associação Cabo-verdiana

A/C Anibal Chantre, R. Acre 55 Sala 100 / CEP 20081, Centro, Rio de Janeiro, Brasil
- Associação Cabo-verdiana

Av. João Firmino, 1443, BairroAssunção São Bernardo do Campo, S. Paulo, Brasil

CANADA
- Associação Cabo-verdiana de Ontario

P.O. Box 14 station L, M6E-4Y4, Toronto, Canada

FRANCE
- Associação Cabo-verdiana de Famek

2 rue St Exupery, B:P: 18, 57290 - Famek, France
- Grupo sem Vaidade

86, Rue Ranelag, 75016, Catt. Cesar Araujo, Paris, France
- A/C Maria Filomena Association Solidarité Cap Vert

Borges, 18 rue Dunoyer de Segonzue, 06200 - Nice, France

- Association Sport et Loisir Franco Capverdien Make-Lovemoiselle
S/C Antoine Monteiro, 41 Rue de Tennis, 57300 — Modelange, France
- M.S.C.V. A/C Luis Pedro Silva, 13 Allé du 19 Mars, 93 Sarcelles, France
- Comite´d'Appui aux Immigrants Capverdiens (C.A.I.CV)
51 Rue des Armandiers, 75020 - Paris

HOLLAND
- Federaçaõ das Organizaçoes Cabo-verdianas de Roterdão
Sgraavendijkwal 144 3015, CD Roterdão, Bangirona 38 19 42 791, Rotterdam, Holland
- União Cabo-verdianda de Amesterdão
A/C Pedro Rocha, Govert Flinckstraat 1108 lll, 1072 - EZ Amsterdam, Holland
- Associação dos Traballhadores Cabo-verdianos na Holanda
Mauritsweg - 19 - 20, 3012 Jr. Rotterdam, Holland
- Comissão Feminina de Roterdão e Comité de Solidaridade com Cabo Verde
Oostmaaslaal 950, 3063 DM Rotterdam, Holland

ITALY
- Associação Caboverdiana
A/C Consulado de Cabo Verde, Via Sanno - 61, INT - 11-00183 - Rome, Italy
- Associação Caboverdiana em Florença e Provincia
Via Chiantigiana -143, C.A.P. 50126 Florence, Italy

LUXEMBURG
- Associação Cabo-verdiana Cultura e Amizade
19 - Rue Michel Welter, 2730 Luxemburg

MOZAMBIQUE
- Associação Caboverdiana
Rua Tchamba 247, Maputo, R.P. Mozambique

NORWAY
- Associação Caboverdiana de Oslo
Postboks 523 Sentrum, Oslo 1 - Norway

PORTUGAL
- Associação Cabo Verdiana de Lisboa

175

Av. Duque de Palmela, nº 2, 8º andar, 1250 Lisbon, Portugal - Tel: 351-21-353-2098-Fax: 351-21-353-2068
• Associação dos Antigos Alunos do Ensino Secundario de Cabo Verde
Rua Manuela Porto, 12-A/12-B Carnide, 1600 Lisbon, Portugal - Tel: 351-21-715-2991
• Associação de Estudantes Cabo Verdianos em Coimbra
Rua Afranio Peixoto, 32A, 3000 - Coimbra, Portugal - Tel: 351-239-26 306
• Fundação Eugenio Tavares
Quinta Nova Sintra - Estrada de Magoito- 84, Casal da Granja - 2710 Sintra, Portugal - Tel: 351-21 961 60 69
• Bios – Associação Internacional para o Desenvolvimento, Medicina Educação em Cabo Verde
Sra. Nominanda Silvestra Almeida Fonseca, Aldeamento das Encostas, lote 27 – Sassoeiros, 2775 Carcavelos, Portugal – Tel:351-21-456 18 30
• ECC-CO
Rua Augusta Nobre 4,2795 Encosta da Portela, Carnaxide, Portugal
Tel: 351-21-418 0875, Fax: 351-21-418 0876
SENEGAL
• Association des Capverdiens d' Origine au Senegal
Rue 9x, Avenue Bourguiba, Villa "Grota de Maria", Dakar, Senegal
SPAIN
• Associação Cultural Amilcar Cabral
Calle Rio Bernesga, nº 15, Bembibre - Leon, Spain
Tel: 00 34 -987- 51 15 55
• Associação Cultural Tabanca
Carretera General 103, 2º dto, Provincia de Lugo, Burela, Spain
• Associaçã Cabo-verdiana de Madrid
C/O Maria Joaquina Rodrigues, Calle Verinica 15, 2º Interior esq., 28014 Madrid, Spain
• Associacion Los Unidos de Cabo Verde
Calle Juan Alvarado - nº 1, 24100 Villabliso, Spain
Tel: 00 34 -87 47 10 31
SWEDEN
• União Caboverdiana em Gotemburgo

A/C Francisco Gomes, Julaftonsgatan 45, 41514 Goteborg, Sweden
- Cabo Verde Association Afremsia Gensration (Club Criol) Friggagatam - 8, 41101 Goteborg, Sweden

SWITZERLAND
- Associação Caboverdiana
B.P. 363, 1205 Geneva, Switzerland
- Associação dos Pioneiros
C.O. Antonio C. Semedo, Croix de Pierre B/6 1470, Estavayer de Lac, Switzerland
- Associação dos Trabalhadores Cabo-verdianos na Suiça
Chez M. Borges Henrique, Avenue Industrie 84 C.P. 1870, Monthey, Switzerland

UNITED STATES
- Cape Verdian Progressive Center
329 Governor St., East Providence, RI 02914-USA
- New England Cape Verdian American Association
64 Charles St, East Providence, RI 02906 - USA
- Cape Verdean American Community Development (CACD)
120 High St. (OFF Exchange St.), Pawtucket, RI - USA
- Cape Verdeans of Southern California (CVSC)
P:O: BOX 8178
Los Angeles, CA 90008 - USA
- United Social Club
480 South Front St., New Bedford, MA - USA
Tel: 1-508-5997-8526
- Fundozinho Lounge
570 Dudley St., Roxbury-Boston, MA -USA,
Tel: 1-617-427-5401
- Ladies Auxilliary
VFW, Dudley F. Brown Post 2846, Ball Park Rd, Onset, MA, 02558
- Falmouth Cape Verdean Club
127 Sandwich Rd (PO Box 2298), Teaticket, MA, 02536
- The American Committee for Cape Verde, Inc.,
14 Beacon St, Boston, MA 02108
- Verdean Vets Hall
561 Purchase St, New Bedford, MA, 02741

- Bomb Shelter

243 Acushnet Ave, New Bedford, MA, 02741

- Cape Verdean Cultural Preservation Council

4013 Annandale Rd, Annandale, VA 22003

- The Main Event Lounge

250 Union St, New Bedford, MA, 02741

- Cape Verdian Artist League

189 -Ives St., Providence, RI 02906 - USA

- Cape Verdian Social Club

1 Vine St, Waterbury, CT - USA

- Santiago Society

84 Talman St, Norwich, CT 06360 – USA

MORE INTERESTING INFORMATION

THE MAP BY JUAN DE LA COSA

This map was made by an officer who sailed on the Santa Maria and accompanied Columbus on his first voyage across the Atlantic. Next to the Cape Verde Islands is the inscription: "Ilha de Antonio" (Antonio's Island) ou del Cavo Verde (or Cabo Verde). This is testimony to the fact that Columbus' crew was well aware of Antonio da Noli and Cabo Verde (The Cape Verde Islands).

EARLY VOYAGES OF COLUMBUS

The 'National Geographic' magazine published a special story on Columbus in 1992 showing a very detailed map of his early voyages before 1492. This map clearly showed Columbus in the Cape Verde Islands and in St Jorge da Mina (Elmina) on the Coast of Guinea in Africa as well as Madeira, all areas where Antonio da Noli was well known and where he exercised tremendous influence. Unfortunately the magazine article has nothing to say about Antonio da Noli and the fact that he governed Cabo Verde and controlled the slave trade in St Jorge da Mina and it is very likely that anyone going to St Jorge da Mina would have had to get authorization from da Noli in order to trade there, since the da Noli family was in control of Cabo Verde and the Coast of Guinea was pretty much an extension of that control.

THE TIME CHALLENGE

In November 1993 Time magazine published a special edition which claimed that the U:S. was becoming the world's first multicultural society and had a computer generated foto of a young lady on the cover.

The woman represented the composition of many different ethnic groups and was labeled as 'the woman of the future'. However, the Cape Verdean Culture Center of Onset, MA decided to challenge the claim and stated very clearly that the Cape Verdean people generated the world's first genuine multiracial and multicultural society which began more than 500 years ago. A decision was made to challenge the Time article and hold a look-alike contest to demonstrate that the

179

hypothetical multicultural woman of the future as portrayed on the magazine cover had already existed in the Cape Verdean community. Then about six weeks later, Mrs. Gina Fontes was selected from among eight contestants as the winner, by an inter-racial panel, which included dignitaries and scholars. It seemed that everyone agreed that Mrs. Fontes has a remarkably striking resemblance to the computer generated woman of the future. Thus the Cape Verdean community effectively refuted the Time magazine article.

ISLAND OF BRAVA, CABO VERDE

On the Island of Brava, there is a town that bears the name of Joao da Noli on top of the mountain, that is a reflection of the direct connection with the town of Noli in Italy and the famous navigator. Joao da Noli was a wealthy merchant and a descendant of Antonio da Noli. Curiously, the only known trace of Antonio da Noli's name in Cabo Verde, is a mountain on the Island of Santiago which is named 'Pico de Antonio' or Antonio's Peak and is believed to be named after the discoverer.

TOURIST AND OTHER USEFUL INFORMATION

BARS AND RESTAURANTS WITH CAPE VERDEAN MUSIC AND FOOD

PORTUGAL
- Discoteca Kussunguila, Centro Comercial Lusiadas – Rua dos Lusiadas, n° 5 (1300 – Lisbon)
- Semba – Discoteca Euro- Africana, Rua Camilo Castelo Branco, 23 – A, Cave (1150 Lisbon)
- Discoteca 'A Lontra', Rua de São Bento, 157, res do chão (1200 – Lisbon)
- B –Leza, Rua da Boavista (in the square of Conde Barão)
- Morabeza – Amadora
Sassassa, Rua Ferreira Lapa, 38 – Lisbon
- A Mormar, Rua Fradesso da Silveira, 75 – Lisbon
- Monte Cara, Rua do Sol ao Rato, 71-A – Lisbon
- Espaço Cabo Verde (Near the Metro – Restauradores)
- Indo- Africa, Rua do Poço dos Negros, 64 – Lisbon
USA
- Caelyn's Kitchen, 35 Depot St, E. Wareham, MA, Tel 508 291 3811
- Pier View Inn (Stevie'sLounge) Onset, MA (Near Onset Pier) Tel 508 291 1649
- Onset VFW, Ball Park Rd Onset, MA

In addition to these establishments, many of the Cape Verdean assocations and clubs have cultural music and a restaurant.

181

ADDITIONAL INFORMATIION ON CAPE VERDEAN CULTURE AND HISTORY

USA

- Wareham Free Library, 59 Marion Rd, Wareham, MA 02571, Tel 508 295 2343 Fax 508 295 2678
- Wareham Historical Society Inc., Captain John Kendrick Maritime Museum, 102 Main St, Wareham, MA, 02571 – Tel 508 291 2274
- James P Adam Library (Special Collection) Rhode Island College, RI
- Cape Verdean TV Productions, Box 9157, Pawtucket, RI 02860, Tel 401 723 7038
- Cape Verdean News (newspaper) PO Box H 3063, New Bedford, MA 02741
- Schooner Ernestina, New Bedford State Pier, PO Box 2010, New Bedford, MA 02741 Tel 508 992 4900 Fax 508 984 7719
- Waltraud (Traudy) Berger Coli MA MBA. (Specializing in Cape Verdean Cultural Research & Consulting), 54 Seaview Ave, Cranston, RI 02905-3616 Tel/Fax 401 781 0021

WEB PAGES AND E-MAIL ADDRESSES
www.capecod.net/~vpires/
www.proudtobecapeverdean.com
www.caboverde.com
www.onsetbeach.com
mbrecords2000@yahoo.com (information on Cape Verdean music)

CABO VERDE

- Instituto Nacional de Cultura de Cabo Verde, C.P. 76 Praia, Cabo Verde
- Tourist Info - CABO VERDE
ALSATOUR,C.P.33 Ponto do Sol – St° Antão, Cabo Verde Tel/fax (238) 21 12 13
- PRALATUR, LDª, 100 Av Amilcar Cabral, CP: 470, Praia – Cabo Verde, Tel(238) 61 57 46/47 fax (238) 61 45 00

PORTUGAL
- Associação Cabo-Verdiana de Lisboa, Av. duque de Pamela, n°2, 8°andar, 1250 Lisbon, Tel 353 2098 Fax 353 2068

ITALY
- Djadsal Holiday Club, Grupo Stefania, via Stretta 28, 25125 – Brescia, Italy Tel 39 (0)30 370 21 88 Fax 39(0)30 39 77 19
- Assessore Turismo, Zolfo Silvio, Comune di Noli, 17026, Noli –(SV), Italy, tel 39 (0)19 749 9532
- Hotel Villa Nina, via Bernizoni, 50, 17028 Sportorno (SV), Italy, tel 39 (0) 19 74 55 47 - This town is about 1 or 2 miles from Noli and highly recommended at very reasonalble rates for anyone interested in visiting Noli.

In addition to the above information, most travel agencies have plenty of information on travel to Cabo Verde as well as many Cape Verdean Embassies and Consulates.

EMBASSIES/CONSULATES
- Embassy, Republica de Cabo verde, 34115 Massachusetts Ave - NW, Washington, DC 20007
- Embaixador, Republica de Cabo Verde, Avenida do Restelo – 33, 1400 Lisbon, Portugal
- Embaixador, Republica de Cabo Verde, 44 Koninginnegracht, 2514 – The Hague (den Haag), Holland
- Consulado Geral de Cabo Verde, 607 Boylston St, Boston, MA 02116 – 3720, USA

CIMBOA

Cimboa is a magazine offered by the Consulate General of Cabo Verde in Boston, MA. It has articles written in Portuguese, English and Crioulo. This is a very informative magazine with many excellent articles on the history and culture of Cabo Verde written by professors and other intellectuals. The price is very affordable for this excellent magazine and it is highly recommended for anyone who is serious about learning more about Cabo Verde and the people of this historic nation.

If you are interested in subscribing to this great magazine, you should contact the Consulate in Boston at the following address:

Consulado Geral de Cabo Verde, 607 Boylston St, Boston, MA 02116 – 3720, USA, email: cimboa@aol.com

Monte Gordo

There is a street in MONTE GORDO, Algarve, Portugal that bears the name "ANTONIO DE NOLA", named after the famous navigator. Monte Gordo is an international tourist town on the sea that is located about 4 kilometers from Vila Real de Santo Antonio. In my discussions with Portuguese historians, it appears that da Noli may have resided in his area during the time that he was preparing to establish the first settlement in Cabo Verde. Prince Henry (da Noli's sponsor) had a castle nearby in Castro Marin, and every year in September, there is a medieval festival in it whereby the local people are dressed in traditional clothing and exhibit the contemporary life stlye. This is a very colorful event and attracts many tourists and highly recommended. There is also a spanish museum nearby in Huelva (Andulucia) that validates the history of Cabo Verde and Portugal along with that of da Noli and Columbus during the 'discovery period'.

Replica of airplane used to cross Atlantic in 1922 by Portuguese pilots (13 days were in Cabo Verde).

This airplane is located in Belem (Lisbon) near the Jeronimos Monastery.Views of the historic town of Noli,Italy. Bottom foto shows entrance to the street -Via Anton da Noli.Postcards of Mindelo, São Vicente,CV. Notice resemblance of the Capitania dos Portos and the Torre de Belem (in a previous postcard of Portuguese Discoveries – both towers have received international funding for renovations)."These coins help commerorate the Treaty of Tordesilhas and the relationship between Cabo Verde and Portugal in this famous treaty made in 1494.

Postcard of Mindelo, Sao Vincente CV. Note the
Capitania dos Portos, which has received international
funding for restoration

Postcard of Mindelo, Sao Vincente CV

188

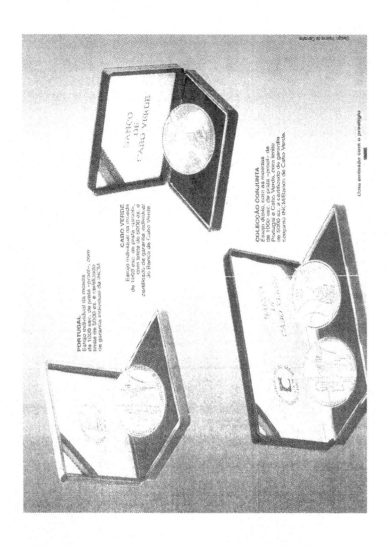

These coins commemorate the Treaty of Tordesilhas of
1494 and the relationship between Cabo Verde and
Portugal.

PORTUGAL • CABO VERDE
DUAS
VALIOSAS
MOEDAS
COMEMORATIVAS

5.º
CENTE NÁRIO
TRATADO DE TORDESILHAS
1494 - 1994

Author's Note

Many more illustrations, maps, postcards and other items that give a flavour of Caope Verde could have been included to highlight the importance of these events that have often been ignored historically and to demonstrate that certain countries recognized the value of these historic events which otherwise would have gone unnoticed.

To demonstrate, especially to the American reader that Cabo Verde has a very important history that has been recognized abroad. This should have meaning especially to the Cape Verdeans in America who should have visual images to associate with their history in order to retain it better. Here we must try to remember that these people were told that the world was divided between Spain and Portugal, but they were never told that Cabo Verde was a decisive factor in this history. Now for the first time they can be made aware of this relationship.

Maps are extremely important for those who want to learn more about this history, whether it is traveling to some of these places or doing research. The reader is urged to use atlases and study maps to place these islands geographically.

Here I must state that there is a new movement that is finally being organized to explore the details of this history and research will be needed to support a new museum which is expected to be built in the next few years. They will need all the help they can get in trying to gather more information.

Hopefully, the images that are included will help promote the tourist industries for these countries, so people will know exactly what they want to see and how to get there. This information will be important to anyone wishing to locate information, especially in the case of those who are planning to fund a museum. That is the current situation in America and we urge all those interested in that project to contact the author.

Comercial ships registered in S.Vicente, Cabo Verde on 31 Dec 1933

Name of ship	Owner
Alcatraz	Manuel Ferreira
Aleluia	Nicodemos Antonio Evora
America	Antonio Miguel de Carvalho & C.[a]
Apolo	Virgilio Carlos Rocheteau
Belmira	Gregorio Gonçalves & Outro
Boa Esperança	Serras& Sousas Limitada
Boganville	Leopoldo e SenaOliveira
Bradford E.Jones	Amalia Monteiro de Macedo
Coriolanus	Pedro Monteiro Cardoso
D. Amalia	Antonio Miguel de Carvalho & C.[a]
D. Maria	Guadencio Antonio Oliveira
Ernestina	Henrique Jose Mendes
Esplendor da Patria	Salomao Benoliel
Fernando	Serras & Sousas Limitada
Fomento	Companhia de Fomento de Cabo Verde
Garça	Benoliell & Bem & Oliel
Ildut	Antonio Miguel de Carvalho & C.[a]
Infante D. Henrique	Governo da Proveincia de Cabo Verde
Irene	Olegario Pedro Ines
Laura São Joao	Joao Jose Pereira
Liberal	Jose Rodrigues Costa
Lima	Miguel Soares Rosa e Diniz
Maria do Livramento	Henrique Carvalho de Sena
Maria Emilia	Serras & Sousa Limitada
Maria Narzolina	Henrique Morazzo
Marne	Tereza Nunes Abrantes
Matiota	Shell Company of Portugal, Ltd
Mensageiro	Antonio Joao Monteiro
Mindelo	Antonio Francisco dos Santos

Mosteiros	Antonio Miguel de Carvalho & C.ª
Nova Cintra	Eduardo Henrique Maia Rebelo
Ondina	Ernestina Neves Morazzo
Palmimina	Miguel Jose Rodrigues & Irmaos
Paul	Lopes da Silva, Limitada
Ponto do Sol	Joao Arrobas Ferro
Porto Grande	Ferro C.ª Limitada
Rapido I	Joao Pereira da Bella
Sagres	Ferro C.ª Limitada
Sal-Rei	Benoliel & Bem Oliel
Santa Cruz	Manuel Semedo Cabral
Santo Antao	Jose Coelho Pereira Serra
S. Jose	Lourenço Jose Ramos & Irmaos
S. Miguel	Manuel Gomes Madeira & Filha
S. Vicente	Serras & Sousas Limitada
Sereia	Julio Bento de Oliveira
Sol Nascente	Ernestina Neves Morazzo
Tarrafal	Viriato Feijoo Pereira
Tarrafal	Ferro & C.ª Limitada
Vitoria	Manuel Gomes Madeira & Filha
Voador	Miguel Soares Rosa
Voz de Cabo Verde	Antonio Miguel de Carvalho & C.ª

Area and Populations of Portuguese speaking countries

Country	Km2	Population
Angola	1,255,755	12,000,00
Brazil	8,511,189	160,000,000
Cabo Verde	4,033	400,000
Guinea Bissau	36,120	1,200,000
Mozambique	801,000	16,600,000
Portugal	92,368	11,000,000
S.Tomé-Principe	971	125,000
Timor	18,989	700,000
	Total	202,025,000

CAGES

We cage ourselves in from what we
dislike or don't understand.
We can transcend the limits of our cage,
when we learn to engage, the "others"
& help them to come out of their cage
& be illuminated to the potential that lies
within their minds,
when it is free to be & see its' ultimate
reality.
White cage, Black cage, it's all the same,
only a name to the game we have been
into for the past five hundred years.
What you see is only a part of me &
you,...we are what we are, but not all we
can be.
Let's look at our history
& see where we would be,
if it had been different & we were really
all one humanity.

Populations of other Lusophone communities (Portuguese heritage)

North America	5-7,000,000
South America	1-2,000,000
Europe	1-3,000,000
Africa	200000
Asia,-Australia	2-3,000,000

Grand Total World Wide(estimated)
211-216,000,000

The Lusiadas- by Luis Camoes

"Arriving in Cabo Verde"

The Lusiadas is perhaps the most famous composition ever written in Portuguese by the world famous author Luis Camoes, however it was not written in Portugal. The works consist of several volumes and they refer to the voyages of the Portuguese navigators in their travels across the oceans of the world and the lands that were encountered during these voyages. Camoes, himself was exiled by the government and wrote his famous works while traveling on these ships during these adventures. And this is just one of the stanzas that he wrote to describe the arrival in Cabo Verde after passing the Canary Islands. It is significant, what he has written regarding the arrival in Santiago, Cabo Verde in stanza No. IX:

"**We are entering the port of one of these islands, whose name was taken from the warrior S. Thiago, The saint who gave a lot of help to the Spanish nation.**"

This is a curious statement, because, the island of Santiago is often written in either Spanish or Portuguese. The Spanish spelling being 'Santiago' and the Portuguese spelling ; Sao Tiago, while in the older spelling it is often seen as S. Thiago. In discussions of this issue with Cape Verdian and Portuguese intellectuals, it seems that 'Santiago' is now being used to designate the name of the island, while S.Tiago or Sao Tiago usually refers to the saint and is often used in matters of a religious nature (in Portuguese). In medieval times both the Portuguese and the Spanish used SANT'IAGO and as the language usage became modernized, SANTIAGO became the accepted usage. Finally, as we have noted earlier, the island was discovered on the day of the saint.

Bishop Pedro Brandao (Cabo Verde)
purchasing slaves in Guinea ca 1600.

Spanish conquistadores in Cabo Verde,
ca 1476.

The Project "Luso Grande do Sul" and the Discovery of Brazil 500 years (1500-2000)

The project 'Luso Grande do Sul' wants to start a broad debate concerning the historical roots of the Luso-Brazilians, returning to a systematic form, to provide indispensable research material to connect future generations with their ancestral past in appraising the Brazilian culture.

This project is being undertaken to celebrate the 500 years since the discovery of Brazil by Pedro Alvares Cabral in 1500 and is being developed by the Federal Universities of Pelotas, Catolica de Pelotas, the University Foundation of Rio Grande, with the help of the Universities of Aveiro, Porto, Coimbra and Lisbon along with other institutions and the first to be presented by the state federation, for three years of festivities for the 500th anniversary of Brazil.

197

The intention is to develop a wide range of intercultural activities at first and in the future to broaden this exchange with other Portuguese speaking countries. Then, by using the most modern means of communications to produce quality material for the commemorations of the 500th anniversary of the discovery of Brazil.

It is clear that the history of Brazil is based on the history of Cabo Verde and a constant continuation of this story. There are opportunities for Cabo Verde and other members of the group of Portuguese speaking nations (CPLP) to amplify this project and to use it as a basis for the education and development of the Lusophone culture.

All of the Portuguese speaking countries should become aware of the other countries, not forgetting the Cape Verdean communities in other countries, such as the United States, Canada, Luxembourg, Angola and Holland, as well as other Lusophone communities. All of the Lusophone peoples have the right to know the way inwhich they are all connected. Not least because the Portuguese language and culture will be strengthened in such a community of nations.

This project was launched in 1996 between Portugal and Brazil. The Lusophone community should investigate this project, and especially, the Cape Verdeans, who have a long history in the development of the history and survival of Brazil since its conception.

"If one does not know his past, he will have a dim view of the future." Baltazar Lopes, Cape Verdean writer

"Life is a book of memories." Marcel Gomes Balla

This book was written in order that we can understand our past, whether we be Europeans, Cape Verdeans, Africans, Indians, Asians, Arabs, Jews, Hispanics or whatever else we may be. I've included a couple of poems from Captain Vasco Pires, because I believe that his words of wisdom help to convey the thoughts of many Cape Verdeans. It is difficult for many people to understand that there are some groups in the world who must challenge the hindrances of being classified as minorities or other nuances while trying to live a dignified life and being all that they can be. Thus I feel that it is important that some of us have the opportunity to see how the world we live in today was really created from the past

500 years or so. In this regard we are all intertwined and can not really escape without carrying the burdens from others as we go about our daily lives.

We should ask our politicians and school boards to review these issues in order that we can reap the benefits of a more inclusive society, whether we live in America , Africa, Europe, Asia or Latin America, it really doesn't matter. What really matters is the need to understand that we are all here for a purpose and that many of our ancestors arrived without their consent and were humiliated in the process. Everybody has a right to enjoy the fruits of his life without harming others. There are many lessons for all of us to learn about human dignity. This is even more important when we realize that we have societies that exist in America and elsewhere in the world today that can provide insight into this area of human behaviour.

THE EYES OF AN EAGLE

My eyes are the eyes of an eagle,

I see above the clouds and through the misty fog.

I see the sins of man, upon the earth below,

And see his future in the path of a storm.

'anonymous'

CONSULATES, VICE CONSULATES AND CONSULAR AGENTS

registered on the islands of S. Vicente
(Mindelo) and Santiago(Praia) in 1899.

Island of S. Vicente (Mindelo)

England	Consulate
Holland	Vice Consulate
Germany	Consulate
Turkey	Vice Consulate
Belgium	Vice Consulate
Austria	Consular Agent
Spain	Consulate
Denmark	Vice Consulate
Russia	Vice Consulate
Brazil	Vice Consulate
Uruguay	Vice Consulate
Peru	Vice Consulate
France	Vice Consulate
Argentina	Vice Consulate
United States of America	Consular Agent
Chile	Consulate
Italy	Consular Agent
Bolivia	Vice Consulate
Paraguay	Vice Consulate
Sandwich (now Hawaii)	Not known

Island of Santiago (Praia)

France	Vice Consulate
Brazil	Vice Consulate
Uruguay	Vice Consulate
Peru	Vice Consulate
Belgium	Vice Consulate
Denmark	Vice Consulate
England	Consular Agent
Argentina	Vice Consulate
Turkey	Vice Consulate
Spain	Vice Consulate
Russia	Vice Consulate

By reviewing this list of consular offices in Cabo Verde it becomes clear that the most powerful nations in the world were registered here in 1899.

A map of 1899 shows the islands at the height of Colonialism, with the world was under the dominance of France, England, Spain, Germany, Belgium, Holland, the United States, Portugal and Italy, all of the countries that were registered in Cabo Verde at this time. So for anyone who should ever say that Cabo Verde is too small to be of significance such as the senior editor of TIME magazine, as was stated earlier in this book, then I suggest that they take a close look at this list.

In fact some countries maintained two offices, so clearly Cabo Verde had to be very important to them.

In 1898 Germany had 247 ships registered in Porto Grande, England had 900, France had 30, Italy had 131 and Portugal had 43 and there were other countries.We should also understand that with so many ships using Cabo Verde, that logically, they have to pay customs duties to the host nation, which in this case, it was Portugal. So why then were the Cape Verdeans so poor and pathetic?

Some Interesting Historical Statistics

The charts depict the aspects of the nature of the Cape Verdean people that is generally unknown.

For example, in 1933, the overwhelming majority of Cape Verdeans were single. Marri age, it seems, was not very popular.

Perhaps this is one (obviously there are many others as we have mentioned throughout this book) of the reasons why many Cape Verdeans have a strong community bond, because they can usually relate to one another in a family atmosphere. Is this good or bad? Only God knows.

Racial statistics were being kept in Cabo Verde in 1933 and the overwhelming majority were designated as 'mixed race'.

This is important to note for those people who happen to be of a mixed race but until now have felt isolated, because they were never officially recognized in any system. I think that it is extremely important for these people to know that they have the right to exist also and that life is a two way street, we must all learn to respect one another.

We must learn to tear down the barriers that have been holding us back and forcing us into isolation. In that regard I stress open dialogue with your teachers, councilors, parents, etc. We all have a right to know who we are and feel like we belong somewhere in this world. Even thieves befriend one another.

Reference: Informação Económica Sobre o Império
Alguns Elementos de Informação Geral
1º Volume
Cabo Verde – Edições da 1ª Exposição Colonial
Portuguesa 1934

Population figures by marital status in selected cities in1933 (Cabo Verde)

City	Total	Men	Women	Single	Married	Widows	Divorced
Praia	5872	2751	3121	5635	210	26	3
N. Sintra	2886	1063	1823	2081	604	194	7
Mindelo	13579	6157	7422	12029	1116	423	11

Note: The overwhelming majority of the population was single in 1933

Racial composition of students in 1933 in selected counties

Counties	Students	Male	Female	White	Black	Mestizo
Total	7856	5144	2712	356	1648	5842
Praia	1024	726	298	67	554	403
Fogo	650	527	123	29	115	506
Brava	493	231	262	147	65	281
S.Vicente	1287	797	490	35	67	1185
Sal	64	31	33	0	0	64

It is very important to note that Portugal recognized the mestizo (mixed race) population.

Registration of ships that entered the ports of Cabo Verde in 1933

PORT	NATIONALITY	No. Merchant Ships
Porto Grande de S. Vicente	German	31
	American	17
	Greek	48
	Dutch	53
	English	178
	Italian	42
	Swedish	15
	Portuguese	55
	Norwegian	25
Praia	German	12
	Portuguese	49

Reference Informação Economica sobre o Imperio, Cabo Verde –Edições da 1ª Exposição Colonial Portuguesa -1934

HISTORICAL COMMEMORATIVES

I've tried to provide in this section some commemorative stamps and other information to simply show that there is certain recognition that has been made regarding the significance of Cabo Verde, especially in the form of stamps and coins for collectors. In fact this is a great way to learn the history of many countries, which are otherwise generally unknown.

I've also tried to bring attention to some historical problems that most European types normally do not encounter in the Western world. Here I'm speaking about the problems faced by dark skinned people on a regular basis. It happens all over the world and no one seems to say or do anything about it and when the people themselves start to complain, they are often accused of exaggerations. A major problem in this regard is that the world is not balanced economically and many dark skinned people have to earn a living in European dominated countries. In fact, much of the European domination is actually in dark-skinned countries where the natives are restless and destitute without much in the way of assistance. But the problem is so bad, we find new revelations every day, that demonstrate a clear fear of non-European types.

Just recently as I write this, the media has reported that 60,000 Swedish women were sterilized so they would not be able to breed and have mixed race offspring. Then I hear about the Jews from Arab countries who feel like second-class citizens in Israel, in fact this complaint has been voiced repeatedly by non-European Jews in Israel.

Amnesty International states very clearly that minority types are treated with a form of international racism that is constantly practised by many European policemen and American policemen.

The standard answer when confronted by these accusations is that it doesn't happen that often. I beg to differ.

It's an international epidemic and it's time that the people speak out!

Hopefully, this book has provided some of the answers to try and solve these problems. Mainly, it is time to focus on the real problem and that is education.

A major purpose of this book is not only to provide historical data that has been obscured in the past, but also to reflect on the real problems that has caused a major imbalance in the way people are seen and treated in this world. Cape Verdeans are not the only ones who have suffered. In fact, in many ways we are all suffering as a result of this ignorance.

It is obvious, that many people are angry, because of their treatment, and when that anger takes over and they can't take it any longer, they start to lose self esteem and self control or perhaps they become criminals and the system says - it's the law and you broke it. Yet much of this anger can be turned around if people are treated more humanely in this world, it does make a difference.

Apparently nearly a half million Blacks are ineligible to vote in Florida because they have a criminal record. Unfortunately many Blacks have criminal records because they are singled out by law enforcement authorities because of their race. Now they can't vote in one US State because they are Black and thus the President of the United States can be determined by the inability of these Blacks to vote.

This definitely appears to be the case in Florida in the Presidential Election in the year 2000 between Gore and Bush. So I hope that there are those out there in society who honestly intend to see to it that people are educated and to help reduce the xenophobia that exists in the world today.

OTHER BOOKS TO READ

The Atlantic Islands: Madeira, the Azores and the Cape Verde Islands, 1971-Duncan T. Bently, Univesity of Chicago

A Portuguese Colonial in America: Belmeira Nunes Lopes, 1923 LATCLEWS – Pittsburgh

Cabo Verde Renascença de Uma Civilização no meio do Atlantico, 1970 – Luiz Romano, Editor da Revista Ocidente – Lisboa
Os Jesuitas e a missão de Cabo Verde (1604-1642) Nuno da Silva Gonçalves – Broteria – Lisboa 1996

Roberto Duarte Silva – um Notavel da Cienca 1942 Carlos Parreira – Colecção Pelo Imperio n° 82 Divisão de Publicações e Biblioteca Agencia Geral das Colonias - Lisboa

Antonio da Noli et lla Colinizzation des illes do Cap Vert in: Miscellanea di storia ligure, III Ed Feltrinelli, 1963 Charles Verlinden

Genoveses na historia de Portugal – Lisboa, in Atti della Sociota ligure di Storia Patria ol XIX Faz 1, 1979

Identidades Reconstruidas – Cabo-verdianos em Portugal, Ana de Saint-Maurice – CELTA- 1997 – Cooperação Portuguesa

Vasco da Gama – O Homem e a Viagem a Epoca –Luiz Adão da Fonseca 1997 –do Comissario da Expo –98 e da Comissão de Coordenação da Região do Alentejo

Web pages: www.caboverde.com
www.onsetbeach.com
www.proudtobecapeverdean.com
www.capeverdeusembassy.org/icpsc.html
"Most Americans know lamentably little
about the Cape Verde Islands and the
contributions of the Cape Verdean
people to the history and devolopment
of the United States." HON. GERRY E.
STUDDS

Other Comments By Lusophones

Reference: Lusofonia - June 1997 - This magazine reports that the Cape Verdean lawyer Germano Almeida from the island of Sao Vicente, "is convinced that Cabo Verde is one of the world's most multiracial countries, even more so than Brazil. He argues that:

"here (in Cabo Verde) no one is linked by this color thing".

He points out that there is a tremendous disparity along social economic lines in Brazil. I've personally been told by friends who know Brazil well, that Blacks, in particular, have difficulty in making economic gains. Almeida then goes on to say that this does not happen in Cabo Verde:

"perhaps, because we don't have anything, it's much easier for us to share it".

Reference: Tchiloli - February 1997 - This magazine from Sao Tome and Principe reports a quote from its director Joao Carlos Silva:

"It is the mixing of races and cultures that we claim as Creoles. Portugal and Angola, continue to this day, to be the entrance and departure points for our grievances to be heard. And it was, especially in these two countries, along with Cabo Verde and Brazil, that our blood has crossed many times: for better or worse.

We are not afraid of history or embarrassed by the past. Because our future has reserved for us a common identity:

that is cooperation in the Portuguese language. The (re) discovery of ourselves so that we can believe in one another and 'achieve things'. The (re) discovery of our ties and relations with one another so that we can forge ahead together. We need to dream to make it possible."

Other Views Concerning Cabo Verde:

The magazine 'Eglise Vivante' dedicated a few paragraphs to the Cape Verde Islands in the review of their world mission in 1956. The magazine states that;

"rarely does anyone speak of this Portuguese archipelago, located west of Senegal"

And it was only by virtue of an appointment by the bishop of Goa who went to the diocese that called attention to the situation and its importance.

It is really a shame that so little is known of Cabo Verde and even less is written about it, because these islands are one of the most important of the original territories of the vast lusophone world and its history and evolution represent some very significant lessons for the world today.

In March 1958, Ricardo Patter, a visitor to Cabo Verde, wrote a special article about his impressions of this land and said;

"It seems to identify itself with Cuba, The Dominican Republic or Panama. During the time that I spent there in Santiago, the atmosphere seemed to be very similar to that of Spanish America (Hispaniola), with its racial mixture, the crioulo flavor, and its high degree of social integration".

This next statement written by a Cape Verdean woman I found to be rather fascinating because it tells a lot about the Cape Verdean people in a way that is otherwise difficult to put into words:

"It is important to know where you come from. We all have something that no other nationalities have. We are all different in color, religion and race, but we are the same people. We are Cabo Verdians. But let us also remember where our father, mother, grandfathers and grandmothers come from. If we don't then we will be like everyone else."

HLM, Massachusetts – She has probably described the Cape Verdean people In just a few lines much better than I have in writing this book.

House of Representatives

CAPE VERDEAN HISTORY

HON. GERRY E. STUDDS
OF MASSACHUSETTS
IN THE HOUSE OF REPRESENTATIVES
Friday, August 2, 1991

Mr. STUDDS. Mr. Speaker, I have the great privilege to represent in this body the Greater New Bedford area—home to the largest Cape Verdean-American community in the United States. Most Americans know lamentably little about the Cape Verde Islands and the contributions of the Cape Verdean people to the history and development of the United States. Mr. Manuel Gomes Baia, a Cape Verdean-American from El Paso, TX, has worked tirelessly to ensure that all Americans are aware of the rich history shared by the people of Cape Verde and the United States. I commend Mr. Baia on his efforts and take this opportunity to share with my colleagues just a few highlights of Cape Verdean history—as provided by Mr. Baia. I am sure my colleagues will agree that we certainly owe Cape Verdeans proper recognition for their role in the development of these United States.

The Cape Verde Islands, known in Portuguese as Cabo Verde, are a chain of islands located off the coast of West Africa. I had the good fortune to visit Cabo Verde for a short time while studying Portuguese and I can personally attest to the beauty of the islands and the graciousness and resourcefulness of the Cape Verdean people. Cape Verdeans have made countless contributions throughout history to the discovery and subsequent development of the Americas, for which they regrettably receive little credit in today's history books.

The Cape Verde Islands were uninhabited at the time of discovery in 1460 when the Portuguese initiated the practice of overseas colonization. New settlements were established on these islands and the settlers in Cabo Verde initially came from Italy, Portugal, and Spain. A few years later, Africa's slaves arrived. Hence, the basis for the evolution and formation of the Cape Verdean people. Today, a majority of Cape Verdeans are known as mestizos or creoles and are a racially mixed group who maintain ties to Europe and Africa as well as Asia and Latin America.

During the 15th century, the Cape Verde Islands were the last known reference points on European maps and thus, a mandatory port of call for great navigators and explorers. Christopher Columbus, Ferdinand Magellan, Vasco da Gama, and Pedro Alvares Cabral all sought logistical support in Cabo Verde before venturing onward.

In 1832, the islands were the first stop of Charles Darwin on his voyage to study "The Origin of the Species," and many historians have reason to believe that Cabo Verde may be the remains of the legendary lost continent of Atlantis.

Cape Verdeans frequently challenged the perils of the seas and eventually sailed their own ships to America. One of the most famous of these Cape Verdean vessels is the *Ernestina* which traversed the Atlantic between Cabo Verde and Massachusetts 52 times under the watch of Capt. Henry Mendes. Because thousands of Cape Verdeans traveled aboard the *Ernestina* to America's shores of freedom and prosperity in the early 1980's, it is as important as the *Mayflower* to the Cape Verdean-American community. Today, the *Ernestina* sits proudly in New Bedford Harbor. It was recently designated a national landmark and is a valuable educational tool and tourist site for students and visitors to southeastern Massachusetts.

Beginning in the mid-1900's Cape Verdeans played critical roles in the development of a lasting economic foundation for southeastern Massachusetts. They were integral in the growth and expansion of textile mills and shoe factories, the cranberry industry, and road development projects.

Several writers deserve recognition for their efforts to preserve Cabo Verde's historic past. Antonio Carreira, of Portugal, has written many books on Cape Verdean folklore and many Cape Verdean writers have produced a wealth of literature which has yet to be translated from Portuguese to English.

UNPUBLISHED INFORMATION ABOUT CABO VERDE NOW PUBLISHED FOR THE FIRST TIME

Significant historical achievements by non-Europeans.

Many of the 'Missing Pages' of Afro and Hispanic American History.

The first non-European knights to be honored by Europeans.

The historic beginnings of the Hispanic peoples in the New World.

The first African society to provide foreign aid to Australia, England, the USA, S. America and many other countries around the world, while changing the economic destiny of mankind.

The first detailed documents published that directly links the Vatican with the Slave Trade.

The first non-European navigators to sail their own boats and make a regular sailing schedule between Africa and America.

A Cape Verdean navigator more important than Columbus? See the first chapter and be your own judge.

The first multicultural society (Africans, Arabs, Jews, Europeans, Asians and Hispanics) that changed the course of world history forever.

CPSIA information can be obtained
at www.ICGtesting.com
Printed in the USA
BVOW03s0838290717
490453BV00001B/5/P